MW00328016

Death By Drama

A Josiah Reynolds Mystery

Abigail Keam

Worker Bee Press

Published in the USA by

Worker Bee Press
P.O. Box 485
Nicholasville, KY 40340

Acknowledgements

Thanks to my editor, Faith Freewoman

Artwork by Cricket Press
www.cricket-press.com

Book jacket by Peter Keam
Author's photograph by Peter Keam

By The Same Author

Death By A HoneyBee I
Death By Drowning II
Death By Bridle III
Death By Bourbon IV
Death By Lotto V
Death By Chocolate VI
Death By Haunting VII
Death By Derby VIII
Death By Design IX
Death By Malice X
Death By Drama XI

The Princess Maura Fantasy Series
Wall Of Doom I
Wall Of Peril II
Wall Of Glory III
Wall Of Conquest IV
Wall Of Victory V

Last Chance For Love Series
Last Chance Motel I
Gasping For Air II
The Siren's Call III
Hard Landing IV
The Mermaid's Carol V

PROLOGUE

The phone rang.

Roused from sleep, Asa leaned over and picked up the receiver on her vintage Princess phone. "Hello?"

Somewhere in the back of her groggy mind, Asa understood that phone calls in the middle of the night were not a good thing. The mental sludge disappeared as Asa focused. Someone was calling on her personal line. That could only mean one person. "Hello!"

"Asa?"

"Mother? What's wrong?" Asa sat up in bed.

"I'm so sorry to call you like this, but you've got to come home on the first plane you can."

"What's happened? Are you in the hospital?"

"Oh, Asa. It's been terrible. No one can get to the bottom of this but you. The police have made up their minds, and there is no talking them out of it."

"Mother, if you don't tell me what the matter is, I'm going to hang up."

"It's Franklin, Asa. He's been arrested for murder!"

1

Asa was still arguing with me as we sat in the back of the courtroom twelve hours after my phone call. She argued with me the moment she stepped off the plane, in the car, in the hallways of the courthouse, and now in the courtroom where Franklin was being arraigned. "Mother, I am an insurance fraud investigator. I specialize in stolen art objects. This is out of my area of expertise."

I gave my daughter one of those "mother looks" and said, "Give me a break."

Asa looked away. "I don't know why you don't believe me."

"Because you are telling a big, fat fib, that's why. Asa, Franklin is my friend."

"I know he is, Mother, but this is something Matt can handle, or better yet, have Walter Neff investigate if you don't think the police are doing their job."

I made a sound that could only be described as a raspberry. "Walter couldn't find a cup of water if he was thrown into a lake."

"Mother!"

"No, you must help Franklin, and that's all there is to it."

Asa started to say more when a basso profundo voice filled the cavernous courtroom. "All rise. The honorable Judge Palton Rosenburg presiding."

We both jumped to attention.

A short, robed figure glided out of a side door, teetered up the steps to the lofty bench, and lowered himself into a sumptuous, high-backed leather chair. Judge Rosenburg was seventy, but still sported a thick head of silver hair.

"You may be seated," boomed the bailiff.

I looked around the courtroom, but didn't see anyone I knew. Hmm.

The prisoners were brought in, including Franklin, who was looking the worse for wear. He sat on a bench and waved when he spied us. He looked scared.

I didn't blame him.

We sat through a mélange of issues—drunk and disorderly, spousal abuse, indecent exposure, and my favorite—urinating in the city's fountains. Finally they got to Franklin's case. He was told to stand before the judge.

Franklin got up and shuffled forward. He shot me a pleading look.

I shrugged back, signaling I didn't know what the holdup was.

"Franklin Wickliffe?"

"Yes, sir."

The judge looked around the courtroom. "Do you have counsel, Mr. Wickliffe?"

"Yes, sir."

"Where is he?"

"I don't know, sir. She was supposed to be here."

At that moment, Shaneika Mary Todd shot through the courtroom door, followed by Hunter Wickliffe, brother of the accused. Matt slipped in behind them, looking quite natty in a navy blue suit and crisp white shirt with a matching blue-gold handkerchief and tie, while the rest of us looked like hell.

It had been a long twenty-four hours since Franklin was arrested. Between giving a statement to the police, calling Asa, and running home to take care of my animals, I barely had time to change my clothes, let alone shower and put on makeup. At least I had run a comb through my red hair. How did Matt always manage to look so good?

I scooted over to make room for him and noticed his face was drawn. For the first time, I detected worry lines around Matt's eyes. Seeing those lines gave me a feeling of satisfaction. So, Matt was mortal like the rest of us.

I guess I should explain who everyone is in this tawdry play. That's how it got started—because of a play. But I'll get to that later. Let's start with the cast of characters.

Matthew Garth is my best friend. He is astonishingly beautiful, and looks like Victor Mature, the '40s movie idol. He is a tax lawyer and lives in a bungalow on my property. He has a new baby girl whom he adores, and the mother is out of the picture for the most part. Think Adonis.

Asa is my daughter. She lives in London, but has an apartment in New York. She has her own company which she insists specializes in insurance fraud, but we all believe she works for the US military, Interpol, CIA or something like that. We're not sure where or for whom, but none of us buy her cover story. My daughter is basically a coiled spring. Think female Dirty Harry. That's my Asa.

Shaneika Mary Todd is my criminal lawyer. Don't curl your nose up at me. Yes, I do need a criminal lawyer from time to time. Doesn't everyone? She is a descendant of the white Todd family and an African slave. Shaneika refuses to say if the Todd family is the same family as in Mary Todd Lincoln, but she wears vintage Chanel suits, displays letters from Abraham Lincoln to Mary Todd's brother, collects Civil War memorabilia, and sits on the board of the Mary Todd Lincoln house. Her office is across from the old slave market in Lexington. Her mother Eunice Todd is my business partner. Shaneika is tough, fierce, and relentless. Think Themis—the goddess of justice who adorns every courthouse holding a sword and scales.

Lady Elsmere is my next-door neighbor. Her real name is June Webster, and she has more money than you or I will ever see. She's an old coot who loves to gossip, but I adore her. I would never have made it through the past five years without her. Think naughty Queen Elizabeth II.

Charles Dupuy (Du-pwee) is Lady Elsmere's butler, and also her heir. Why is her butler an heir to a massive fortune? Well, Charles is not just any old butler. He is the scion of Aaron and Charlotte Dupuy, slaves of Henry Clay. Remember Henry Clay from your history books? He is still considered the greatest statesman the US ever produced, and is often referred to as the Great Compromiser. Just think how powerful and intimidating Henry Clay must have been, but that did not stop Charlotte Dupuy from legally suing Master Henry for her freedom. She lost her lawsuit and was sent into the Deep South as punishment. Later, Henry Clay relented and freed both Aaron and Charlotte. Since Lady Elsmere doesn't have any children, and she loves Charles and his family, it was a no-brainer. After all, Charles' family helped build this great nation. Why shouldn't they have a piece of the money pie? Think James Earl Jones.

Hunter Wickliffe is a forensic psychiatrist and Franklin's older brother, who moved back from London to take over the family estate. They are from an old, aristocratic Lexingtonian family, and Hunter is trying to save his family home, which is a crumbling antebellum mansion—think Tara from *Gone With The Wind* after the War of Northern Aggression—that's Southern code for the Civil War.

He and I have been seeing each other from time to time. I don't know where it's going, and I don't think he does either. If I was going to cast Hunter . . . let me think for a moment . . . yes, think Clark Gable.

The last of this casting call is Franklin—the accused. I first met Franklin through Matt when I was in the hospital several years ago. Since then, we have grown close. Franklin is bright, witty, and bodacious. He has an apartment in Lexington, but spends most of his time at Matt's cottage, helping with the baby. Franklin loves to go through my clothes and throw out my "granny pants" underwear. I'm just glad I haven't caught him *wearing* my granny pants underwear. Franklin is like a flower. Yes, Franklin is a sunny yellow flower blooming on a chilly spring day. Think daffodil.

And then there's me—Josiah Louise Reynolds. I'm a beekeeper, and I live in the Butterfly, a mid-century marvel. I make my living by selling honey at the farmer's market and renting out my house for events. A few years ago, I was injured falling off a cliff and have serious health problems, but get this—I was about to go under financially until the money I got from a lawsuit due to the fall saved my home. Now try this on for irony. My injuries have resulted in declining health, which means I might not get to enjoy my farm for long. Boo-hoo. Poor me. And another thing—I've been stumbling over dead bodies for several years now. I seem to have a knack for it. Think of a wisecracking Jessica Fletcher. She's sugar. I'm spice.

Let's see—where did I leave off? Shaneika was standing with Franklin in front of the judge. Hunter was sitting behind them.

"So glad you could join us, Counselor," the judge said, peering over his glasses.

"I'm sorry, Your Honor. I'm ready to proceed."

"Mr. District Attorney, I'm waiting," the judge complained.

"The Commonwealth of Kentucky charges Franklin Wickliffe with murder in the first degree for the death of Madison Smythe."

I gasped. First-degree murder can mean the death penalty in Kentucky.

Matt grabbed my hand as his face drained of color.

"How does your client plead?" asked the judge, looking at Shaneika.

Shaneika frowned at the prosecutor.

Franklin, in shock, mumbled, "What did he say?"

Recovering, Shaneika said, "We plead not guilty, sir."

The prosecutor sniffed.

"Very well. Bail is set at $100,000 dollars," intoned the judge.

"Your Honor. We feel the prisoner should be remanded into custody. He is a serious flight risk," the prosecutor asserted.

Shaneika interjected, "Your Honor. My client is a respected member of the community. He has never been charged with a crime before—not even a parking ticket. He has deep roots in the community—a job, family, a home."

"Your Honor. Madison Smythe was viciously murdered, and the Commonwealth will prove that Franklin Wickliffe was the culprit."

Shaneika grinned at the Prosecutor, as though saying "I'm gonna eat you for dinner, boy." Throwing shade at the DA, Shaneika complained, "Your Honor. It is not even clear if Madison Smythe was murdered. The DA's office is jumping the gun here. There's no witness to this supposed murder. No weapon. There's no evidence of any kind."

The judge pushed his glasses back up on his nose and glared at the DA. "Is this true?"

"Your Honor. There are witnesses who will testify that Franklin Wickliffe threatened Madison Smythe, saying he wanted her dead. She was a healthy young woman with no medical problems, and then she died in Franklin Wickliffe's ancestral home after a confrontation with the defendant."

"Save it for the trial, Counselor, but if the ME's report states that Mrs. Smythe died of natural causes, the Commonwealth has opened itself up for a lawsuit by the defendant. You'd better have your ducks in a row."

Hunter stood up. "Your Honor. Franklin is my brother. I will personally take responsibility for him."

The judge peered over his glasses at Hunter. "I recognize you, Mr. Wickliffe. You have testified in my court."

"Yes, Your Honor. I am sometimes hired by the local police."

"I remember." The judge leaned forward in his chair while perusing the docket. "Very well, then. Franklin Wickliffe is remanded into his brother's custody pending posting of bail. Mr. Wickliffe, you are to surrender your passport to the court. Trial will be set for September 30th." He briskly rapped his gavel on the massive oak bench and ordered, "Next case."

Franklin gave Hunter a bewildered glance as a bailiff led him away. He seemed utterly helpless and confused.

We followed Shaneika into the hallway.

"Where're you going, Hunter?" I asked, pulling on his jacket.

"To post Franklin's bail," he replied over his shoulder as he sped down the hallway to catch up with Shaneika.

I didn't take offense. Hunter had been under a lot of strain since yesterday. He was bound to be on a short fuse today. What I didn't expect was for Asa to observe our interaction so closely.

"Is that Franklin's dad?" Asa asked.

"It's his brother."

Asa leaned over and whispered, "I didn't even know Franklin had a brother."

"Shush. He always said he had a brother."

"Yeah, but I thought he had died or something. We never saw him, and Franklin never talked about him."

In case you're wondering—no, I hadn't told Asa about Hunter. Well, there's no use talking about a new relationship if you're not sure there is a relationship. If Hunter was *just* going to be a "friend," what would be the point of discussing him with her? Hunter's away so much, consulting as a forensic psychiatrist, that it's hard to get him revved up. When Hunter comes home, he's tired and needs to rest, or he wants to work on his house. I can understand that. We're not kids anymore, but shoot, I want a fire. It doesn't have to be a blazing fire, but some glowing embers now and then would be nice.

Oh, blah, blah, blah. Yes, I know my health is declining, and I should take it easy. I'll take it easy when I'm six feet under. Right now I'm still breathing and moving—so let's get on with it.

But I never mention my feelings to Hunter. Why? Because I don't think I'm a great catch. Like I said— my health is declining. I'm not much to look at, either. Passable. My daughter scares people. And my friends are eccentric, and that doesn't include my new hobby—stumbling over dead bodies all the time. I come with a lot of baggage. I'm grateful that any man who has a job and his own teeth wants to spend any time with me at all, so I'm not going to rock the boat.

2

Hunter unlocked the door to his dilapidated mansion and threw his briefcase on a chair by the door. He had spent a great deal of the day at the bank trying to get a line of credit on the farm so he could bail Franklin out of jail.

The bank said no.

The farm was in sad shape. There were no crops in the fields and no horses in the barns, mainly because the fields were fallow and the barns were falling apart. Tobacco was a thing of the distant past. Heirloom tomatoes were the mainstay crop of Bluegrass landowners now, and Kentucky was the largest producer of beef cattle east of the Mississippi. The only problem was Hunter knew nothing about tomatoes or cows.

Hunter had an emergency account of four thousand dollars plus his salary, which depended upon someone hiring him as a consultant. It could be feast or famine, depending on the needs of law enforcement. That was it. What savings he did have, Hunter had invested in the farm. That had gotten the house up to livable and the driveway drivable—just barely. Blast it! Why hadn't he saved more?

After the brush-off at the bank, he and Matt went to lunch, trying to figure out a way to spring Franklin from the hoosegow, but Matt was tapped out as well. He had spent his money on recovering from a bullet wound, refurbishing his house, and now, with a new baby, he was broke—also living from paycheck to paycheck. Hunter broached the question. Could Matt ask help from his baby's mother, Meriah Caldwell, the famous mystery writer?

"Yes, I can, but I know what the answer will be," Matt replied. "A big fat no. She hates Franklin and thinks he is one of the reasons for our breakup."

"Oh, I didn't know the situation was so messy between you and my brother."

Matt shook his head. "It's complicated, and that's all I'll say on the matter."

"What about Josiah?"

"She adores Franklin, but she barely has two nickels to rub together after paying her monthly bills. The smart thing to do would be to sell the Butterfly, but Josiah is determined to keep her land out of the hands of developers or die trying. There's no money there."

Hunter felt his gut tighten. That left the banks. Circle right back to a dead end.

3

After another discouraging bank visit, Hunter was exhausted and wanted nothing more than to have a glass of bourbon—lots of glasses filled with bourbon—eat something and fall into bed. Tomorrow he would start again to look for money to bail Franklin out.

Hunter had started up the massive staircase when he heard the unmistakable clink of ice cubes falling into a glass. "Hello? Anyone there?" he called out, wishing he had a gun. Pulling an umbrella from a brass stand near the door, he fumbled in his pockets for his phone. Rats!

He had left his phone on the passenger seat in the car, and to make things worse, he didn't have a land-line.

Now was the decision to confront or run. Was he a man or a mouse? Twenty years earlier, Hunter could have easily answered that question, but his reflexes weren't so fast, and it had been a long time since he was in a brawl.

But who was in his house? It couldn't be Franklin, since he was still in jail. Wasn't he?

The front door was locked when he came in, so it had to be Franklin. A robber wouldn't break in and then lock the door.

Hunter strode into the parlor with umbrella pointed in front of him—just in case. "Franklin?"

Instead of Franklin greeting him, a stunning young woman sat in one of the wingback chairs, comfortably sipping his expensive bourbon.

"Are you going to stab me with your umbrella?" the woman asked.

"Who are you, and what the hell are you doing in my house?" Hunter peered closer at the woman, who was wearing skin-tight black pants, and a black top with long sleeves and V-shaped collar. He noticed she wore military-type boots.

"Wait a minute," he said. "I saw you with Josiah this morning." He pointed a finger at her. "You're her daughter, Asa."

Asa nodded.

"I don't mean to be rude, but what are you doing here? How did you get in?"

She held up a little black case. "Professional picks. Tools of the trade."

Hunter was utterly astounded. "You need to explain yourself, or I'm going to call the police. Did your mother put you up to this?"

"Mother doesn't know I'm here, but she did call and beg me to help, so here I am."

"Do you always pull stunts like this?"

"Like what?"

"Entering people's homes without a warrant and going through their things."

"I don't use warrants. I'm not a cop. You weren't home, so I let myself in. I thought you might want my help. I'm like my mother. I'm very good at solving puzzles, but if you don't need me, then I'm off to London again." Asa rose and set her glass down on a table.

"Wait a minute, Batgirl," said Hunter, gesturing for her to sit back down. "You startled me, that's all. Please stay. It's been a rough two days, and I'm out of sorts."

Asa stayed on her feet.

"My apologies for calling you Batgirl, but you must admit the only thing you're missing is knee-high vinyl boots."

"You are not endearing yourself to me, Mr. Wickliffe."

Hunter ran his fingers through his thick hair. "I don't know what I'm saying. I'm flummoxed. Franklin and I were gobsmacked by this arrest. I haven't slept since it happened. Please, please sit."

"I must admit you weren't supposed to find me here. You came home sooner than I expected."

"What were you looking for?"

"Just inspecting the scene of the crime. After all, a woman died here under the most excruciating circumstances. I wanted to check the room without someone hovering over me."

"I heard that you do things. How shall I put this?"

"Not quite by the book, as they say?"

"Exactly."

Asa responded with a self-satisfied smile. She sat down, reached over, and picked up her bourbon. "That's how I always catch the bad guy."

"Do you always catch the bad guy?"

"I've nabbed my fair share over the years."

"If my brother's freedom wasn't at stake, I'd pitch a fit at this intrusion into my privacy."

"But you won't, because you know I might be useful." Asa looked at her watch, slowly took a last sip of her drink, and rose. "I must be going. Mother is expecting me for dinner, but I'll be in touch, Mr. Wickliffe. There are a few holes in your story that need clearing up. Ta-ta." Asa swept out of the parlor and out the front door, leaving Hunter Wickliffe rubbing his chin in bewilderment.

4

"Where have you been?"

"Went to check out the scene of the crime."

"Was Franklin's brother there?" I asked.

"You mean Hunter Wickliffe?"

"Yes," I replied, not trying to sound too curious. "What did the two of you talk about?"

"What do you mean?"

"It means Miss Josiah shouldn't ask Miss Asa too many questions. How many times have I told you there must be plausible deniability?" Shaneika fussed, strolling into the great room of the Butterfly.

I threw my hands up in the air.

Asa and Shaneika bumped fists.

"Something smells mighty fine, Ma. We be having biscuits?" Asa said with a Kentucky mountain drawl.

Shaneika declared, "You're very cheeky tonight."

Asa turned toward her. "Why are you here, anyway?"

"That's a fine how-dee-do. I want you to know I

gave up a date at a very exclusive restaurant to eat with your *ma*."

I interrupted, "Shaneika needs my statement. You need to hear it too, so I thought I could kill two birds with one stone. Sorry about your date, Shaneika. I didn't know. Was it with Mike?"

Shaneika grinned. "Yeesss."

Smirking, Asa threw a small couch pillow at her. "Look at you. Getting serious."

I finished setting my Nakashima table and put on my mother face. "Come on, girls. Wash your hands and let's eat."

"You don't have to tell me twice," Shaneika replied, rising.

Asa followed her into the kitchen, only to stop and plant a wet one on my cheek.

I fondly watched her dutifully wash her hands.

Of all my daughters, she was my favorite.

That's a joke, y'all.

5

We sat down to a house salad with homemade ranch dressing, a tomato-cheese quiche, sliced strawberries and oranges plus warm blackberry muffins.

"Sorry, girls. I didn't feel up to preparing a big meal. This will have to do."

"This is fine, Mother," Asa said, slathering butter on a muffin.

Shaneika nodded her head. "You don't see my plate empty, do you?"

"Where's Linc tonight?" I asked Shaneika about her son.

"He's with Mother. They're going to a movie later on tonight."

"That's nice," I replied, wiping my mouth with a vintage lace napkin. I detest the current custom of using paper napkins at the dinner table. "I hope when Linc grows up he loves his mother enough to live close, and not move to another continent."

Asa made a face at me.

Shaneika rose to get a legal pad and pen. "All righty then, I'm ready if you are, Josiah," she said sitting back down.

I cleared my throat. "Well, I'm part of an amateur theater company."

"When did this start?" Asa asked.

"Over a year ago. It was something to do in the evenings."

Shaneika inquired, "You act on the stage?"

"It isn't a group like that. We perform on location in places like borrowed mansions or a city park for a couple of nights. It's rather informal. We invite our friends. We do it for fun."

"Do you charge for this?" Asa asked, amused.

"Just a nominal charge to cover the cost of the refreshments."

"You ask your friends to witness these plays, and then make them pay for their own cookies and Kool-Aid?" Asa chided.

"We happen to serve passable wine and whatever stinky cheese is on sale. We're very good, Asa, if you must know."

Shaneika cut in, looking amused, "Now, Josiah, tell the truth."

"Well, the director said I have no stage presence, and I couldn't deliver a line on a silver platter, so now I'm the wardrobe mistress, which is crap, since the actors don't wear costumes. I help Franklin, who is the props manager. He also acts in small parts like a waiter or the butler."

"Oh gosh, the butler did it," Asa giggled.

I protested, "Asa, this is serious."

Asa shot a glance at Shaneika, trying to reel in another accomplice, but Shaneika only stared back with indifference.

"Sorry, guys," Asa muttered. "I'll be good."

"I'll continue then, if I may. Well, the director, John Smythe . . ."

"Smith? Seriously? John Smith? You gotta be kidding," Asa echoed. "How drab."

"They dress it up by replacing the 'i' with a 'y.'" I was getting irritated with Asa. She was not taking this situation seriously.

"Do they put an 'e' on the end?"

I nodded.

Asa snorted. "Pretentious."

Shaneika turned to Asa. "If you interrupt your mother one more time, you'll have to leave the table. You are being disrespectful. A man's life is at stake. Not just any man, but one of your mother's dearest friends. A first-degree murder charge is nothing to sneer at."

Asa batted not an eyelid nor flinched from shame. "You know as well as I do that this whole thing is ridiculous. Franklin couldn't hurt a fly."

"The police don't think so," I countered.

"Who's the idiot in charge of this case anyway?"

This was the moment I had been dreading, but I coated my answer with as much venomous honey as possible. "Why, darling, it's your old boyfriend, Officer Kelly."

6

A rookie knocked on Detective Kelly's glass door and poked in his head. "There's a woman here to see you."

Kelly looked up from his paperwork. "Who is she?"

"She wouldn't tell me her name, but she's a looker."

"By all means, send her in."

Kelly stood up and straightened his tie. "Oh, no," he whispered as he recognized the tall woman sauntering toward his office. Kelly drew in a sharp breath.

As he watched her approach, he wondered why she had none of Josiah's Scandinavian coloring or features. She was the spitting image of her father Brannon. Dark, brooding eyes, pouty, full lips, and thick, glossy brunette hair that fell below her shoulders. Patrician features. By heaven, Asa was a stunner, and the older she got, the more beautiful she became.

Kelly felt a painful longing and then piercing guilt. He had a wonderful wife and children. Yet he dreamed about Asa. Damn it! Asa was his albatross, the one person who could trip him up and ruin his life. Suddenly Kelly felt a surge of hate for her.

Why had she come back? *Asa, go away. Go away!*

"Hello, Officer Kelly."

"It's Detective Kelly."

Asa inclined her head in acknowledgement, taking in the surroundings of his cramped office. At least he had a window. "May I sit?"

Still standing, Kelly barked, "What do you want, Asa?"

If Kelly's brusque manner bothered her, Asa gave no indication of it. She slowly lowered herself into the chair opposite Kelly's cluttered desk and crossed her legs, showing off her "kiss-me" red stiletto high heels.

Although half the squad in the warren of cubicles was rubbernecking to steal a glance into his office, Kelly tried to behave nonchalantly. He straightened his tie again and sat down. "To what do I owe the pleasure?"

"Mother is convinced Franklin Wickliffe is innocent."

"I beg to differ. Only Franklin's fingerprints were on the decanter and the goblets. He had both motive and opportunity."

"You're saying Madison Smythe was poisoned?"

"No comment."

Asa scoffed. "Have you taken a good look at Franklin? He wouldn't harm a snake if it bit him, let alone poison a woman."

"He was overheard by members of the cast saying he hated the victim and could kill her."

"Oh, and I guess you've never said you could kill someone when you were mad."

"He made credible, specific threats. Don't forget those fingerprints."

"Yeah, what about them? He was the props manager. Of course his fingerprints were all over the wine decanter and goblets. I'll tell you whose fingerprints weren't on the glassware—the real murderer, because he wore gloves, trying to pin this on Franklin."

"Franklin will have his day in court."

"He should never have been arrested, and you know it."

"Asa, you're trying my patience."

"Did you look at possible lovers? Life insurance policies on the victim? How about that husband of hers? I hear they had some take-no-prisoners fights during rehearsals."

"You know I can't comment."

"Okay, be that way. I'll undertake my own investigation."

"You can't do a thing. You have no PI license for Kentucky."

Asa rose. "Au contraire, mon ami. I do, and it is up-to-date." Before going out the door, Asa asked, "How's your wife?" Making sure all the men were having a good look at her, Asa blew Kelly a kiss.

Without realizing what he was doing, Kelly grabbed it.

7

"Tell me the entire story, and don't leave anything out," Lady Elsmere, aka June Webster, instructed.

I had been invited or rather summoned to afternoon tea at June's residence, affectionately known as the Big House. "We were in the middle of dress rehearsal when Madison Smythe started acting intoxicated."

"That's John Smythe's wife?" asked Charles, who was serving tea before a roaring fire in the library. After handing me a teacup, he served himself and sat, joining us. Truth be told, Charles loved gossip as much as we did.

"Yes. She's the star of the play, and her husband John is the director."

"You mean 'was,'" Charles said.

June asked, "What was the name of the play?"

"*The Murder Trap* by Abigail Keam," I replied.

Charles ventured, "That's a tricky play to stage properly, even by a professional group."

"Who else is in your little troupe?" June asked. "I socialized with Madison and John. Anyone else I might know?"

"There's about twenty of us, but you go to church with Robin Russell and her husband Peter."

June thought for a moment. "He's the college biology professor who's always crying poor-mouth. Someone should tell him it's rude to discuss money in public."

"That's him," I concurred.

June pursed her lips.

"Zion Foley is another one of our members. You know him."

Charles declared, "His family owns a winery in Woodford County."

June huffed. "I don't drink domestic wines."

"Do you want to hear this or not?" I fired back. I knew for a fact that June drank Zion's wines. She was just being ornery.

Both June and Charles nodded.

June pantomimed zipping her mouth shut.

"You don't know the others who were there. There was a young woman named Deliah Webster, and a new player by the name of Ashley Moore. The rest of the actors hadn't arrived yet."

"Go on," Charles encouraged.

"Very well, then," I said, before taking a genteel sip of tea. "Like I was saying—Madison started acting loopy and said she felt funny. We had her lie on the couch. John seemed annoyed the rehearsal had been interrupted and demanded to know if she'd been drinking. Madison got indignant and said no. I went to the kitchen to get her a drink of water and a cool hand towel for her forehead when I heard shouting from the parlor. Franklin bolted out the back door to fetch Hunter, and I rushed back to see Madison had fallen on the floor and was convulsing."

Charles held up a finger.

"Yes?" I said.

"So Hunter was not taking part?"

"No. Franklin had gotten permission to use the house and furniture. Hunter consented as long as we didn't break anything."

"The decanter and the goblets were his?" June asked.

"Those items were from the Wickliffe estate."

June waved her hand. "Continue."

"John tended to Madison. I called 911. Hunter ran in with Franklin on his heels. Hunter checked Madison's pulse and administered CPR, but when she didn't respond, he checked her vitals and declared her dead."

"This sounds very much like Addison DeWitt's death in my house," June mused, pulling a cigarette out from her cleavage.

Charles reached over and grabbed it. "Old woman, you know you're not supposed to be smoking. You got any more down there?"

"You wanna look, old man?" June replied, looking defiant.

"Hey! Hey! Behave, the two of you." I gave June a stern look. "If you smoke, I'm going to leave."

June reached into her décolletage and produced two more cigarettes, which Charles promptly snatched. "Well, it does sound like Addison DeWitt's murder," June muttered.

"I don't think Madison was allergic to aspirin," I replied, looking at June's chest and wondering if she had even more cigarettes stuffed in her brassiere. I shuddered to think what else might be crammed in there.

"I thought you said she was convulsing," June snapped, looking as though she had caught me in a lie.

"She had been, but by the time Hunter got to her, she'd stopped and was still."

"Then what happened?" Charles asked, his eyes a little too bright.

"One of the actors drove to the front gate and opened it for the ambulance. Other than that, we just stood around in shock. Hunter lifted Madison back onto the couch and got John a brandy."

June remarked, "Is that when Franklin said, 'It couldn't have happened to a nicer person?'"

"How did you know?" I asked.

June picked up a shortbread cookie. "Isn't that why

the police started looking at him as a suspect?"

"Why am I telling this story if you already know what happened, June?" It pissed me off that she always had the scoop before I could relate my version of the story. It had happened many times before, and was extremely exasperating. Did this woman have a spy ring at her command?

"I only know the essentials, Josey. I need you to add the juicy details."

Charles waved his hand, intending to shush June. He wanted to get on with the story. "Why did Hunter put Miss Madison back on the couch? He knows better than to disturb a body that's been murdered."

"We didn't realize Madison Smythe had been murdered at this point. The consensus was her death was due to natural causes."

"Who called the police?" asked June, while peering down her bosom. What was she going to pull out next?

"The paramedics called the men in blue," I replied, getting ready to swat June's hands away from her boobies. "What are you looking for?"

"My handkerchief. It's down here somewhere."

"May I, Lady Elsmere?" Charles said. For a horrifying second, I was afraid Charles was going to fish around in June's bosom in search of the lost hanky. Thankfully, he reached into his jacket and produced a crisp, white linen hanky.

"Lady Elsmere, huh? What happened to 'old woman?'" June barked as she took the handkerchief and blew her nose.

Charles turned to me. "What do you think happened, Josiah?"

I shook my head, saying, "I don't know, Charles. I was blown away when I learned the police suspected Madison's death was due to poison."

"Did they say what kind of poison?"

I scooted closer to Charles on the couch. "The ME's report hasn't come back, so it isn't officially ruled poison yet, but if it was poison, it wasn't strychnine. That's a nasty one, for sure. I would think Madison seeming intoxicated is a clue, but I would hesitate to say for sure until the medical examiner's report is completed."

"Why arrest Franklin before the tests come back?"

"That's what I've been asking. It's not like there's a lack of suspects. There's something the police are not telling anyone except the DA."

"What do you mean, Jo?" June asked, handing the dirty handkerchief back to Charles.

He stuck it in his coat pocket and asked, "Yes, why is that?"

"Oh, everyone hated Madison's guts. She was a first-class witch."

June scoffed, "Don't hold back, Josey. Tell us how you *really* feel."

"Don't act like a hypocrite. You never liked her

either," I said, making a face at June.

June looked at her butler and heir. "Mister Charles, what about you?"

"Shouldn't speak ill of the dead."

"Oh, you are always so polite," June complained, looking irritated. "How can Josiah solve this murder if we don't face the facts as they are? No one liked Madison. Jo's right. I couldn't stand her."

Charles asked, "But what about Franklin?"

"That's why she called me!"

We all snapped our heads toward the door.

In strode Asa wearing a very tight black dress with red piping and shockingly tall high heels the same red as the piping on her dress. She threw her purse into a chair and plopped down on the other side of Charles, giving him a buss on the cheek. "May I have some tea, please?"

Charles was only too happy to oblige. He had a soft spot for my errant daughter and always had. "Glad to see you, Miss Asa."

Asa cooed, "It's a good day when I can rest my eyes upon you, Charles Dupuy."

June griped, "What about me?"

Asa got up and went around the coffee table, curtsied, and kissed June's hand. It was a running joke between them. When Asa was little, she thought June was a queen because of the tiara she wore to parties. She sat in a chair next to June and reached for the cup

Charles handed to her.

I asked, "Well?"

"Went to see Kelly, but he was not very forthcoming."

"As was expected," I commented.

"It seems that the only incriminating evidence is Franklin's fingerprints on the decanter and goblets, and the testimony of witnesses who overheard the argument when he threatened to kill Madison. Personally, I agree with the judge. The police jumped the gun on this case and have opened themselves up to a lawsuit. He did confirm they think Madison died of poison."

"Don't they have to disclose all their evidence to the defense attorney?" Charles inquired.

"They probably will when the test results from the autopsy come back. I'm sure they aren't finished looking for evidence. I would expect Hunter Wickliffe to be served with a search warrant any moment now, and the police will turn his place upside down."

"Eeek," I muttered before stuffing a raspberry brownie down my piehole.

"I've never understood what caused Franklin to threaten Miss Madison," Charles said. "He's always such a friendly person."

"I can comment on that," I said. "I heard the entire argument and paid it no mind. It was just two diva cats letting the fur fly."

Asa, June, and Charles leaned forward.

"Madison was getting on everyone's nerves. She had the lead role, and you'd have thought she was preparing for an Oscar."

"Wouldn't it be a Tony since it was a play?" Asa asked.

"Oh, fiddle-faddle, Asa. Don't derail my train of thought." I sat still for a moment, collecting my confidence. You know my memory isn't what it used to be.

"Let's start with why you didn't think anything about the argument," Asa encouraged, sorry she had interrupted her mother. (She had recently discovered her mother was having trouble with her memory. She had also gone through Josiah's medicine cabinet and found a new medication that had to do with kidney issues, at which point Asa decided to tackle one issue at a time with Josiah. First, it would be Franklin. Then the new medication. Now, on with the story.)

"Like I said, Madison was acting like she was sittin' in high cotton. Bossy, rude, demanding with everyone, and John running after her like she was the Queen of Sheba."

"Mother—you're bossy."

I retorted, "Yes, but I'm not rude when I'm bossy."

Asa tried not to smile. "I've talked with several of the cast, and they said Madison Smythe always knew her lines, hit her marks, and was professional. It seems her problems were with you and Franklin."

June and Charles swiveled around to gauge my reaction.

"Well, gee, that's true to some extent. Franklin and I seemed to be on the receiving end of her disregard, but others were unhappy with her constant bickering and complaining, too. They're lying if they say different. Everyone was fed up with her high-handedness."

Asa made a note to re-interview those cast members she had talked with. She was getting two versions of Madison Smythe's character, and when an investigator got varying stories, that meant someone was not telling the truth, and she doubted it was her mother. Josiah was unusually perceptive about people, except when it had come to Asa's father, Brannon. There had been a huge blind spot with him until Brannon wanted a divorce. Then the scales fell off her mother's eyes, but with others, she was always right on target. Well, maybe she missed with her friend Sandy Sloan, too, but Asa hadn't seen the warning signs either. "Go on, Mom. Sorry."

"Madison insulted Franklin constantly, not outright, but with backhanded compliments like 'Franklin, you're so handsome. Too bad about your choice of attire.' Or she'd say, 'I heard about Matt Garth and Meriah Caldwell. Too bad you're always the bridesmaid and never the bride.' She was always needling him, and knew just where to jab."

"Did Franklin confront her?" Asa asked.

"Not at first. He would ignore her, but Madison kept it up. She was like a dog with a bone. Several times I took her aside and told her she was rude, especially since we were using Franklin's ancestral home to stage the play, but Madison laughed it off. Then she started goading me as well."

Charles inquired, "To what do you attribute her behavior?"

"I think she was jealous."

"Jealous?" echoed June.

"I think so. Madison was a climber, and she thought Franklin was beneath her on the social ladder. Then she found out Franklin is part of the old Lexingtonian aristocratic past with the family lineage and estate still intact. I know it's run-down, but Wickliffe Manor is still very impressive. And the mansion's paintings, antiques, and silver are worth a small fortune."

"The problem is, nobody wants antiques anymore," Charles sniffed. "The young people want cheap furniture from kits they put together themselves."

"Madison was envious of Franklin because of his social position," repeated Asa, making note of this information.

"I hate to add this, because there's no proof, but I think she also objected to Franklin being gay, because she couldn't control him like she could heterosexual men," I said.

"Did she try to control Hunter Wickliffe?" asked

Asa, looking intently at me.

"Yes."

"Did Hunter Wickliffe respond to Madison's flirtations?" Asa inquired, still not taking her eyes off me.

"I never saw any indication of it. He always found an excuse to work in the yard when she was present."

"Then I wouldn't repeat that. It makes you a target."

"Why?"

"It gives you motive."

"I don't know what you mean."

"I'll say it again. It gives you motive. Hell hath no fury like a woman scorned."

I guess Asa had put two and two together and guessed about Hunter and me. "My lips are sealed."

June complained, "Go on. Go on. Enough about Hunter. I want to hear about the argument."

I continued. "It came to a head when Franklin accused Madison of stealing some sterling salt and pepper shakers from the dining room table."

Asa asked, "Did she?"

"Yes."

"How do you know?"

"While they were arguing, I checked her coat, which was hanging in the foyer. They were in her left pocket."

June inquired, "What did you do?"

"I yelled that I had found them, but didn't say where."

"Did the fighting stop?"

"Madison was furious with Franklin, but he was just as angry because he insisted other items were being spirited away from the house."

Charles asked, "Did Franklin see Madison take the salt and pepper shakers?"

I shook my head. "When items previously went missing, Franklin had surreptitiously checked people's coats and purses, and always found the items in Madison's coat pockets. He would put them back where they belonged. After all, this was his brother's home, and Franklin felt an obligation to Hunter."

"Did Franklin accuse her in front of everyone?" June asked, rummaging inside her blouse for another cigarette. As soon as she produced one, Charles snatched it away from her.

"He made a snide remark that all actresses must be kleptomaniacs like Natalie Portman."

Asa remarked, "It was Winona Ryder who was arrested for shoplifting."

"I know, but I'm telling you what Franklin said. Madison snapped, 'Are you referring to me?' and Franklin said, 'If the shoe fits,' and it escalated from there."

"Tell us more," encouraged June breathlessly.

"Franklin accused Madison of stealing bits and pieces from the house. She yelled back that Franklin was a liar and trying to spread horrible rumors about her. Franklin called her a tawdry, backstabbing tart."

Charles gasped. "He said that?"

I replied, "That's when Madison slapped Franklin's face, and he blurted out that he could kill her."

Asa insisted, "Tell me what Franklin said, Mom. Exactly."

"Franklin said, 'I wish you were dead, Madison. The world would be better off.'"

"The exact wording, Mom. He didn't say he wanted to kill her?" Asa asked.

"It's the same thing."

"No, it's not, Jo," June interjected. "Stating that you wish someone was dead and making the threat to kill him are two very different threats. For most of us, it's wishful thinking.

"We've all had people in our lives we wished were out of the way, but I doubt anyone in this room has planned to murder someone, except for Asa, of course."

Asa made a face. "Ha Ha."

A triumphant grin lit up June's face.

"Mom, what happened after the confrontation?"

"Hunter made Franklin apologize in front of the entire company. Madison accepted, and they shook hands."

"And?" Charles demanded.

I shrugged. "As you would expect, everyone was polite, but the tension was so thick . . ."

"You could cut it with a knife," everyone sang in unison.

Asa rose and said she needed to get back to the Butterfly.

"Not staying for dinner?" June asked, looking downcast.

"No, my dear. I've got to write down all this information. I promise, though, to see you again before I leave."

June flapped her hand. "Phooey."

Charles glanced over at Lady Elsmere and said, "Lady Elsmere, where is your emerald ring? You had it on earlier."

June looked around. "Oh, dear, it must have slipped off my finger."

"I'll help you find it," Asa said, getting on the floor and feeling under the couch.

Charles and I checked under the cushions while June checked the stuff down her blouse.

"Here it is," she announced cheerfully, holding up the ring.

Asa peered down June's blouse. "What else do you have in there? There could be a treasure trove of goodies."

Charles assured us. "Don't worry. I'll have Amelia go through her clothes. She's missing a platinum bracelet as well."

We laughed, including June. It's good to have a sense of humor in these situations.

Charles showed Asa and me to the kitchen door and

bade us a cordial farewell.

Asa and I walked across the fields, but as soon as we were out of earshot, Asa let me have it.

8

"You're not telling me everything."

"I don't know what you mean." I didn't want to get into it with Asa. I was tired, but Asa could be relentless, and it seemed I couldn't deflect her.

"You're holding something back."

"No, I'm not."

"Mother, you're lying."

"Oh, all right. When I checked Madison's pocket searching for the salt and pepper shakers, there was something else."

"What?"

"A note."

"What kind of note? Did you read it?"

"This is your mother you're speaking to. Of course I read it. I think it was a love note."

"You think? Mother, please stop playing this game. Give. What did the note say?"

"Darling, we'll be together soon."

"Now we're getting somewhere. Did you leave the

note in Madison's pocket?"

I shook my head, afraid to look Asa in the eye. She was going to think I was an old fool.

Asa looked at me oddly. "Franklin called Madison a tart. He's never judgmental about anyone's sexuality, except for adultery. Did he think Madison was having an affair?"

"Yes. He had found other love notes in Madison's pockets when he was searching. They were communications about clandestine meetings, love poems, that kind of thing."

"Let me put this together. Franklin told you what he found, but why would he care?" Asa picked up a fallen branch and threw it back into the woods. "Were the notes typed or handwritten?"

"The one I saw was handwritten."

"There you go again—holding something back." Asa thought for a moment. "You recognized the handwriting."

"I thought it was similar to the handwriting of someone I know."

"And Franklin did too. That's why he was upset. It must have been Hunter's handwriting. You both thought Hunter was having an affair with Madison Smythe."

I stopped and burst into tears.

"Mother, are you sweet on Hunter Wickliffe?"

"I like him very much."

"Why would you lose sleep over a man who cheated with another man's wife? You went through this with Dad."

"I can't believe Hunter would have anything to do with a creature like Madison." My voice was crackly.

"Men are dogs. You know that. Why didn't you mention the note to the police?"

"Because I took it."

"That was Franklin's free ticket out of jail. John Smythe could have known about the affair and killed Madison."

"It also points a finger at Franklin. It would explain why he disliked Madison so much, and why he would have killed her to protect his brother."

"Very weak motive. John Smythe is a better candidate for murder. Husbands are always the prime suspects in a wife's murder. Then again she could have ended it with Hunter, and he killed her out a fit of pique. Some men don't like to be rejected."

"Hunter would never," I protested.

"Please don't tell me you destroyed the note."

"No, I didn't destroy the note," I replied in a whiny voice. "I'll take the note to Kelly tomorrow and get Franklin out of jail."

"Don't. I want Franklin to stay right where he is for now. If he was out, he would be buzzing around me like a guard bee, giving me no rest. I need to concentrate on this case. It's starting to unravel, and it may unravel in a way you might not like, Mom."

"What should I do with it?"

"Keep it tucked away for now."

"I feel so stupid."

Asa put her arm around me and squeezed. "You don't feel good, do you? I can tell."

"I need to check on the bees," I said, not wishing to discuss my health.

"I'll go with you."

Asa and I went into the bee field and did a quick perusal.

"Mom, look," said Asa, pointing to fecal stains at hive entrances.

Dark brown stains spotted the entrance to the some of the hives.

"Jumping Jehosaphat! Looks like they have dysentery. This is bad," I said, examining all the hives. About four were in bad shape. Madison Smythe would have to wait. My bees needed me.

Honeybees are very clean creatures. They like an unsoiled hive, so they potty in fields on "cleansing runs." Diarrhea in honeybees is very serious. Dysentery can be caused by a multitude of reasons, like too much cold weather, bacteria, or water inside the hive, or even tainted honey. If the colony wasn't taken care of fast, it could collapse, and the condition spread to the other hives.

Asa and I hurried home, where I boiled some sugar

water into a thick syrup and mixed it with medication after it cooled down. We then took the medicated syrup and opened the infected hives. Everything smelled and looked normal. I couldn't find evidence of anything to cause the illness until I pulled out one frame, and saw it was covered with mold. I took it out and put in a frame with fresh beeswax. I would take the moldy one home, scrape the moldy wax off the insert, and soak the frame in disinfectant.

I checked the other hives, but found nothing to explain this condition. That's how it is with beekeeping sometimes. You scratch your head, wondering. As a precaution, Asa cleaned off the entrance boards with a mild disinfectant and then rinsed with water.

I would check the bees again in a couple of days. If the bees were still sick, I would have to up my game and call the state bee inspector for help, but at the moment I had done all I could.

And the emergency got Asa off my back. At least for now.

9

"You again."

"It looks like the police did a thorough job," Asa said, looking around the front parlor that Hunter used as an office.

"I locked my gate. How did you get in?"

"Very easily, Mr. Wickliffe, if you know how."

"Call me Hunter. Mr. Wickliffe is my father."

"Okay." Asa had learned from her mother never to call an older person by their first name unless she had permission. It was rude, but then so was breaking into someone's house. Asa had to make choices sometimes.

"Find anything yet to clear my brother?"

"Working on it."

"And?"

"May I see a sample of your handwriting?"

"What for?"

Asa gave a wicked smile. Her teeth were startlingly white, even, and original—not veneers. It was obvious that Josiah had spent a fortune on an orthodontist when Asa was in her early teen years. "You want me to help your brother or not?"

"I don't see how my handwriting could have anything to do with Madison's death."

"You're refusing?"

"No. No. Just don't see how it would help." Hunter went over to a massive rosewood desk. "What do you want to see?"

"Handwritten letters. Canceled checks. Journal entries. Calendars, notes, those kind of things."

Hunter gave Asa a curious look, but pulled out his checkbook from a desk drawer. Lifting his briefcase off a chair, he gathered his calendar and case notebook and placed them on the front edge of the desk before plopping in a wingback leather chair.

Asa compared the handwriting from the note her mother had given her to the handwriting in the documents on the desk.

While Asa studied the material, she asked, "Did the police ask you for a handwriting sample?"

"No. Should they have?"

"Did they ask you to take a polygraph test?"

"No. Say, what are you getting at? What's that paper you have?"

"Hush for a minute. I'm just about finished."

Hunter opened his mouth to argue but thought better of it. If this irritating young woman could help his brother, he was going to cooperate. He sat back in his chair and watched her compare the handwriting on the paper to the writing in his personal items. Where was she going with this?

Asa took a small camera out of her pocket and photographed pages from his case notebook.

Hunter protested, "Stop. That information is confidential."

"It's for my own use. No one else will lay their eyes upon it."

"Miss Asa, this most annoying."

"I'm sure it is. You know what I do for a living?"

"Your mother says you are some kind of international cop."

"My mother exaggerates."

"I don't think so in this instance. Franklin told me he saw a video on YouTube where some army nurses are singing and goofing around, but you are in the background with a briefcase chained to your wrist, talking to some muckety-mucks in a jeep, and the terrain looked like Iraq. The video has since been taken down.

"Also, Matt told me that when your mother fell off the cliff, you arrived in a military helicopter with several men who appeared to be Special Forces. You didn't allow anyone to talk with them before they flew off. Now, I find these stories rather peculiar."

"I am hired by insurance companies to investigate fraud, mainly stolen or forged artworks—paintings, rare books, coins, that kind of thing."

"Uh-huh."

"I'm very good at my job, Hunter. I can spot a forgery a mile away, and this is not your handwriting," Asa said, holding up her piece of paper.

"What is it?"

"How well did you know Madison Smythe?"

Usually it was Hunter asking the questions, and he didn't like being on the other side of an investigation. Still, he answered, "I didn't. Just enough to say hello."

"How long had you known her?"

"I met her and the rest of the theater group when Franklin asked if they could use the house for their play."

"Did you know any of the other players?"

"Besides Franklin and your mother, no. I've been living in England for a long time and only recently came home. Most of my old friends are living in Florida or California. Very few of the old gang are still here."

"What was your relationship with Madison or John Smythe?"

"Like I said—just on a hello basis."

"What did you think of Madison?"

"She was a pretty woman with some acting talent."

"Is that all?" Asa pressed.

"What more should there be?"

"Franklin thought she was stealing expensive items

from the house. Did he confide this to you?"

"Yes, but I didn't take it seriously."

"Why not?"

"It was obvious Franklin didn't like her."

"Perhaps he didn't like Madison because she was stealing."

"He told me to lock up the silver, and I did."

"Franklin said that on the night of Madison's murder, a sterling salt and pepper shaker went missing. My mother found them in Madison's coat pocket along with this note." Asa tossed the note over.

Hunter picked the paper up and studied it. "This is a photocopy?"

"Yes."

Hunter read the note and murmured, *"Darling, we'll be together soon.* What does it mean?"

"That's what I would like to know."

Hunter guffawed. "You think I wrote this. Believe me when I say Madison Smythe was not my type."

"What type would that be?"

"Married."

"Is my mother your type?"

"None of your business."

"My mother's welfare is my business. I'm going to ask you again—are you seeing my mother?"

"Ask her. What do Josiah and I have to do with this tragedy?"

"I know my mother didn't kill Madison Smythe, but

I'm not sure about you."

"I was not seeing the woman." Hunter wanted to get back to Josiah. "Did Josiah say something about me?"

Asa smiled. "She didn't tell me anything about you, but the note bothered her. She recognized the handwriting."

"How many times do I have to tell you? I didn't write it."

"I believe you, but you have to admit the handwriting is quite similar."

Hunter started to say something, but Asa cut him off. "As I said, I can spot a fake right off. The handwriting looks like yours, but is not. I will have an expert verify my conclusion, but it looks like someone was trying to set you up, and my mother bungled it by taking the note. It was supposed to be found by the police, but Mother had it in her purse."

Hunter looked thoughtful. "Does your mother think I killed Madison?"

"If I were in your shoes, I would be focusing on who would want to target you."

"I'm more worried about Josiah."

"I would be upset if someone hurt my mother."

"I can see you're very protective. Truth be told, though, we haven't seen much of each other lately."

"Why not?"

Hunter glanced about the room. "This place takes

every nickel I make, and I'm not making any headway in preserving it. It's a money pit. I've been taking any case thrown my way. Between working and trying to get this place back on its feet, I'm too tired to romance your mother, Madison Smythe—or any woman, for that matter."

"You might want to explain the situation to my mother. I believe she thinks you're not interested."

"So you want a man to tell a woman he's too old and too tired to make her happy? Jeez, why don't I just slit my throat?"

"Sell the place."

"Hell, no! And let some greedy developer get their hands on this property? No way. This is the Bluegrass. God doesn't make any prettier country, and I'll do all I can to preserve this land for future generations." Hunter paused for a moment. "I sound rather grandiose, don't I? The truth is I might have to sell the estate, and the thought is killing me. With Franklin's attorney's fees, I might go under if I don't sell, but I'm finding it difficult to even think about it."

"You sound like my mother."

"She's got her head screwed on straight when it comes to preserving the land. I take it you don't agree."

Asa ignored his question and segued back to the murder. "If Madison was having an affair, whom would you suspect?"

"I haven't a clue. I paid very little attention to the goings-on of this theater group."

"No idea at all? Never noticed anything? Heard anything? A man in your profession would observe little things most people would never see."

Hunter shook his head.

"What about John Smythe?"

"I'm sorry. I can't help you."

"What are you going to do about Franklin?"

"I have a meeting with another bank in the morning. Matt and I are going together."

"All you need is ten thousand to make bail. He only has to be liable for the $100,000 if he skips court. Surely Franklin has 10k tucked away somewhere."

"I know the law. Franklin's bail doesn't concern you."

"I think there's something fishy about you and Matt not finding the money to get Franklin out of jail. In fact, I think there are things you aren't telling me, but I will find out, Hunter Wickliffe, what those secrets are."

"Please see yourself out."

"I guess that's my cue to leave."

Hunter remained passive in his leather chair.

Asa threw him a brilliant smile. "You think Franklin killed Madison, don't you?"

"I think nothing of the kind."

"As I said, I can see a fake a mile away, and that includes lying. I'll go, but I'm going to get to the bottom of this murder. You can count on that, Hunter Wickliffe. You can surely count on it."

10

Franklin eased into a jailhouse chair. "Asa, I thought I saw you at my arraignment."

"I was there."

"It was nice of you to come." Franklin looked around sheepishly and lowered his voice. "Any idea of when I'm getting out of this horrid place?"

"Matt and your brother went to a bank this morning. Nobody's heard from them yet. They've been having trouble raising the ten thousand."

"The silver in the house is worth ten times that. Can't Hunter put it up as collateral?"

"There's a problem. People aren't buying antiques or silver tea sets these days. There's a glut on the market. Young people aren't interested in remnants of the genteel past, so the bank may not want to accept them as collateral."

"What about the land?"

"I think you're going to have to have a long talk with your brother about that when you get out. The farm is upside down."

"What do you mean?"

"Hunter has sunk about every penny he has into the family estate, and he's drowning in debt."

"That can't be. My brother makes a fortune with consulting. He should have more than enough money."

"Your brother had several divorces before he came home, which cost him quite a bit, and then it is taking him a long time to build up a clientele in the US. To be blunt, Hunter is not making the kind of money he made in Europe."

Franklin's face drained of color. "I asked him about the farm, and he said everything was okay."

"Of course he did. Hunter's your older brother. He doesn't want you to know he's floundering."

"I've been so preoccupied with Matt and the baby, I guess I wasn't paying attention. I thought he was fine because he bought the Hanoverian for himself and a pony for your mother."

"Hunter bought Mother a horse?"

"So Josiah didn't tell you, huh?"

"There's a lot my mother isn't telling me."

Franklin's eyes darted to the floor.

Asa took quick notice of it. People look away when they're fibbing or don't want you to know that they know something. It's an automatic response.

"Franklin, I found a new medication in Mother's medicine cabinet. You know anything about it?"

"No," replied Franklin, his face turning a healthy shade of pink.

"Franklin, I flew all the way from London to help you, so this is quid pro quo. Squeal, or I'm taking the afternoon flight back to England."

Franklin panicked. "Don't tell her I told you."

"Cross my heart."

"She's having trouble with her kidneys."

"I thought as much. What kind of trouble?"

"I don't know exactly. She won't discuss it with me. I found the same medication in her bedroom. When I confronted her, she told me her kidneys were acting up, and I was not to tell anyone."

"Does Matt know?"

"I don't think so. If Matt did, he would insist on going to the doctor with her, since Josiah has been forgetting things recently."

"I've noticed this too since I've been home."

"I think the memory loss is caused by the kidney issue. I looked it up and found toxins not removed by the kidneys could cause memory loss."

"I see my stay is going to be longer than I anticipated, but let's get on with first things first. I need you to tell me exactly what happened on the night of the murder."

"Let me think. Everything has been quite a blur since then."

"Get on with it, Franklin. Quit stalling."

"Oooh, you don't have to be that way."

Asa gave Franklin a stern look.

"I got there early to prepare the room, since this was a final dress rehearsal. I placed the furniture on their marks and then went into the kitchen to get the decanter ready."

"What does that mean?"

"I poured cranberry juice into the decanter and placed it in the fridge."

"Did you always use cranberry juice?"

"Yes, it looks just like cabernet. Then I placed the goblets on the table."

"Was the juice bottle sealed or opened?"

"Unsealed. I had used it several nights before for the play."

"Did Hunter ever drink from the bottle?"

"No. I mark the level and label that it's for the play. Besides, Hunter doesn't like cranberry juice."

"Was the color of the juice the same?"

"Meaning what?"

"Was it lighter or darker?"

"The same, I guess. I didn't notice."

Asa made a mental note of this. "Okay, then what did you do?"

"I placed the goblets on the table."

"Had the decanter and goblets been cleaned?"

"I washed them the other night and left them on the drainboard."

"Did you put anything in the goblets?"

"No, I just put the empty goblets on the table, as I told you."

"Which table was it?"

"The magazine table."

"Describe it to me."

"Early twentieth century. Black walnut with inlaid poplar. It sits on a pedestal that rotates, and has four slots under the top."

"So you can put different materials in the slots and rotate it while you're sitting in your chair to get to the slot you want. I remember seeing it."

"That sums it up."

"Why use that table?"

"John insisted on it."

"John Smythe?"

"Yes."

"Is that kind of table described in the script?"

"No. Prop instructions call only for a small end table."

"Then what did you do?"

"I went out to see Hunter. He was already working in the backyard."

"What was he doing?"

"Yard stuff. Gathering fallen branches, raking up debris. That kind of thing."

"Did you help him?"

"Couldn't. I heard commotion in the house and

went back in. John liked to start exactly on time, and I wanted to make sure everything was in order."

"Who was there?"

"John was in the kitchen. He took the decanter into the living room and filled the goblets. Madison was smoking on the front terrace. Zion Foley and Robin Russell were rehearsing their lines in the dining hall. The other players hadn't arrived yet."

"My mother?"

"Josiah's always late."

Asa took note of this as her mother was usually punctual.

Franklin hesitated a moment, then continued. He wasn't sure what Asa was looking for. "I noticed the table with the decanter and goblets was dusty, so I took everything off, dusted, and replaced the glassware."

"Did you place the goblets in exactly the same places?"

"Sure."

"Now think, Franklin. This is important. Did you put the goblet that was placed on the left back on the left?"

"Well, I don't remember." Franklin pantomimed taking the goblets off, dusting, and then replacing them. "It's possible that I switched goblets. I'm not sure. Is it important?"

"What kind of decanter and goblets were you using?"

"Nineteenth-century Venetian ware with gold trim around the lip and stem. My great-grandmother purchased them on her grand tour in Europe."

"Was this the set always used for the play?"

"Yes."

"Is there anything that distinguishes one goblet from the other?"

"There are eight goblets in the set, but I always used the same two because they looked shabby. Some of the gold trim is worn on one side of a goblet that was used. The other one has a small chip on the base. I didn't want to use the nicer goblets."

"Was anyone else near the table?"

"I wouldn't know. I was in the other rooms making sure all the valuables were put away."

"In that case, how did the salt and pepper shakers end up in Madison's coat pocket?"

"I wish I knew."

"Before your blowup with Madison, whom did you confide in about your suspicion that she was stealing?"

"Josiah. I mentioned something to Hunter but didn't go into detail. Just said to lock everything up."

"Okay, that's all for now, Franklin." Asa started to rise, but Franklin grabbed her arm.

"When am I getting out of here? I only have to pay $10,000 to get out. Why am I still here?"

"You'll have to talk to your brother about that . . . and speak of the devil, here he is."

"I hope you have good news," said Franklin, looking back and forth between Asa and Hunter.

Since Hunter seemed reluctant to speak in front of her, Asa took her cue and left. She looked back to see a disgruntled Franklin angrily gesturing at Hunter, who seemed very uncomfortable.

Apparently another bank had said no.

11

Matt had to work, and his babysitter bailed on him, so I ended up with the little bundle of stale milk breath and poopy diapers. I had just put the baby down to nap when I heard the doorbell ring.

Who could that be? Asa had a key, and I had recently changed the code to the driveway gate.

I tiptoed to the front and glanced at the monitors. Oh, Lord, it was Meriah Caldwell with a policeman! What was Meriah doing here? She was supposed to be in Europe researching her next book. And why would she need a policeman?

I opened the door and stood in the doorframe. "Meriah? Can I help you?"

"I stopped at Matt's bungalow, but nobody was home, so I thought Matt might be here."

"During work hours? You know he went back to his firm."

"May I come in?"

"No. What's with the cop?"

"I thought Matt might not let me see Emmeline."

I gave Meriah a curious look. "You know Matt will let you see Emmeline whenever you want. He's never been contentious about your visitations, however infrequent." I just had to get that dig in.

Something was not right. Meriah shows up out of nowhere with a cop when she knows Matt is at work. She was up to something.

"Is my baby here, Josiah?"

"No."

Of course, right after I lied, the baby started crying.

Both Meriah and the cop heard her. "You do have Emmeline!" Meriah tried to push me aside, but I held my ground. She was actually tussling with me to get past. Jumping Jehosaphat!

"Meriah, what are you doing? What's going on?"

"I want my baby, and I want her now."

"I'm sorry, but until I know what's happening, I can't let you see her."

"I'm taking her, Josiah, and you are not going to get in my way."

"Do you have a court order? Does Matt know about this?"

"I'm her mother, and I want her, so I'm going to take her."

"Meriah, calm down. Matt will be home in three hours. Why don't you wait at his home, and the two of you talk this through? If you want to see more of the baby, I'm sure Matt will be more than accommodating."

"I have a plane to catch, and the baby and I will be on it."

"You mean to California? No. No. I can't allow that to happen." I looked over her shoulder at the cop standing a few feet away. "Officer, this woman does not have legal custody of this baby." I looked into Meriah's angry face. "If you take Emmeline, you will be arrested for kidnapping. Think of what you're doing, Meriah."

Meriah shoved me and kicked my shinbone.

The policeman did nothing to help, just watched stupidly until something very large, brown, and furry lunged past me and knocked Meriah down and sat on her.

BABY TO THE RESCUE!

"You put that gun away!" I yelled at the cop.

"It's a lion," he said, his pistol shaking in his hand.

"It's an English Mastiff, you idiot." I was madder than a wet hen and smacked the door with my hand so powerfully that the doorframe shuddered. I bellowed in a voice that could be heard clear across the Kentucky River. "IF YOU TRY TO TAKE THIS CHILD, I'LL COME DOWN ON YOU SO HARD, IT WILL BE LIKE THE HAND OF GOD SMITING YOU! NOW GIT! BOTH OF YOU!"

I pulled Baby back into the house and slammed the

front door, locking it. Then I ran to secure all the back doors. I had my patio doors open to the pool, and barely got them closed and locked before I saw Meriah and the cop barreling onto my back terrace. I closed the drapes and called Matt. Of course, he was in a meeting and couldn't be reached. I fumbled with my old-fashioned rotary phone and called the Big House.

Ring. Ring. Ring. Ring. Ring.

"Come on. Come on. Someone answer the damn phone," I muttered.

"Hello, darling," June's voice sang from the phone.

"June!"

"You sound out of breath, dear. What's wrong?"

"June, is Charles around, or any of the grandsons?"

"He's out in the back pastures, checking on the foals."

"I need him, June. Fast. Meriah's here, and she's trying to steal Emmeline, and I can't get hold of Matt. I need reinforcements. Now!"

"Where's Asa?"

"She's not here. Do you think I'd be calling you if she was?"

"Don't be insulting, Jo. Hold tight. I'll get Charles. Don't worry."

I hung up in a frazzled state. Not knowing if Meriah was calling for more police reinforcements, I grabbed Baby and went into my bedroom, where I locked the steel door shut and got out my taser.

The baby was screaming now, probably due to all the noise. I picked her up and swaddled her in a blanket. "There, there, Emmeline. Don't cry."

Unnerved by Meriah, who was now pounding on the back windows, Baby growled and paced back and forth with his hackles up. The noise agitated Emmeline, making her cry louder.

"Baby, lie down. Lie down," I commanded my dog.

Baby totally disregarded my commands. It was his job to protect, and that's what he was going to do, even if it meant making things worse.

I started to cry. Yes, cry. I can't handle stressful situations anymore. The least little thing sets me off. With both Emmeline and me crying, I was running out of handkerchiefs. The only critter not bawling was Baby, who was howling.

Would Meriah ever stop pounding on the windows? Good luck trying to break them. They were bullet-proof.

A chair was thrown against one of them. Oooh! If Meriah damaged one of my good patio chairs, I was going to make her pay through the nose.

I thought about calling the police myself, but decided against it. Cops are quick to act when a baby is involved. Meriah is a famous person, and if she told the police she had custody, they might storm the Butterfly to get the baby before the truth was worked out. By that time, Meriah could be on a private jet with Emmeline, flying out of the country.

Finally the pounding stopped.

Baby stopped howling and looked at me, as if asking what he should do next.

I shrugged. I was too busy calming the human baby to pay much attention to the canine Baby. He poked his nose through the drapes to take a peek.

"What do you see, Baby? Is Meriah gone?"

Baby looked back and forth between the drapes. Suddenly, he rushed to the bedroom door, barking and jumping up.

There was a slight tapping on the door, and someone tried to turn the doorknob. I heard a muffled "Mom, are you in there? It's me. Unlock the door."

I rushed with Emmeline in my arms to open the door.

There stood Asa with Charles. Both looked baffled.

Asa said, "I just passed Meriah and a cop flying down the driveway. I had to pull over to let them pass, and then I meet Charles rushing over through the pastures." Asa shot an irritated look at Emmeline. "Can't you shut her up?"

"Your compassion is overwhelming." I handed the baby over to Asa. "Here, you try to soothe her. I need a drink." I marched into the great room and poured myself a neat bourbon. "Charles, do you want one?"

"No thanks. I would love to stay and hear what just happened, but I've got four-legged babies of my own to see about. Everything okay here? I can leave?"

I sank into my sofa cushions and took a long sip before answering. "Yes, of course. June said you were checking on the foals. Asa's here, so I'll be fine. Thank you so much for coming to my rescue, Charles."

"Anytime, Josiah."

"Make sure the front door is locked behind you," I called out as Charles was leaving.

"Asa," I called out. "ASA! ASA!"

Asa came into the great room. "Quiet. I just got the rug rat to settle down."

"That's great, but you're going to have to get her up again. I need to see a doctor."

"What for?"

"I think I broke my hand when I struggled with Meriah."

Jumping Jehosaphat!

12

My hand wasn't broken, but the little finger on my right hand had a hairline fracture. I was now home with my pinky in one of those metal finger thingies. The doctor had given me a pain shot, though, so I was a happy girl.

However, Matt was not a happy boy. He was pacing and mumbling, "Why would Meriah do such a thing?"

"You're wearing a path on my carpet."

"You have no carpet."

"It's a figure of speech. Please sit down. You're making me dizzy."

Matt harrumphed but plunked down beside me.

"I warned you Meriah might change her mind about wanting the baby. She definitely was going to kidnap Emmeline. And there's another explanation."

"What's that?"

"Meriah could be suffering from postpartum depression."

"I thought of that. I'm very concerned for Meriah,

but she won't answer my calls."

"Be expecting a lengthy custody battle."

"I can't afford one."

"Here's another thought. She heard about Franklin's murder charge and thinks Emmeline is better off with her. Meriah never liked Franklin, you know."

"That's putting it mildly. I never understood why. Franklin's such a pleasant person."

"You know, Matt, for a bright man, you're kind of stupid sometimes."

Matt pulled me close and kissed my temple. "Ah, you say the sweetest things to me."

We clung to each other for safety, our friendship a barrier against the dangers from the outside world.

And I didn't let go.

13

I must have dozed off, because I woke up on the couch with a blanket thrown over me. I guess that pain shot knocked me for a loop.

The Butterfly was quiet, and it was dark outside. I stumbled around until I found a light switch. To my surprise, there were all sorts of baby things in my great room: playpen, several suitcases, toys strewn on the floor, diaper bag, bottles, etc.

I guess Asa and Matt had come to some sort of agreement while I was conked out, and Matt was apparently staying at the Butterfly. I didn't care at the moment. My pain shot had worn off, and my little finger was throbbing. I got up and staggered in search of my secret stash of pain pills.

In my bedroom where I kept my stash, slept Asa and Matt, with Emmeline and Matt's dog Ginger between them along with a bowl of half-eaten popcorn. Lying at their feet was Baby, sawing logs, with various cats sprawled on top of him. Asa must have let the

Kitty Kaboodle Gang inside.

I turned off the TV. They had been watching *Charade* with Audrey Hepburn before they drifted off.

Both Asa and Matt looked exhausted.

I put a blanket over them both and took Emmeline with me. I was afraid they might accidentally roll over on her.

Baby lifted his head and opened his good eye. "Go back to sleep," I whispered.

I went to the guest bedroom, where I found a crib and Matt's toiletries. I put the sleeping baby in the crib and set the alarm clock, climbing into bed fully clothed.

I wasn't going to wake the household rummaging for my illegal stock of pain medication.

My throbbing finger would have to wait.

14

The next day I met Matt at Shaneika's office.

Shaneika listened patiently to me as I spelled out what happened with Meriah at the Butterfly yesterday. She tapped her pencil eraser quietly on her desk until I ran out of breath.

"Matt, I'm not a child custody lawyer, but Meriah may very well have legal grounds to take Emmeline away. After all, Franklin does spend a considerable amount of time with her, and he's now charged with first-degree murder. If I were her mother, it would give me pause, and a family court judge might see things the same way. However, based on Josiah's testimony, Meriah acted in a rash and unstable manner, trying to kidnap the child."

Shaneika put her pencil down and leaned forward, resting her forearms on her desk. "I've already filed two restraining orders against Meriah for you both, and a judge who owed me a favor has already signed them. Josiah, I would suggest you report her attack to the police and press charges for wanton endangerment. Make sure you take pictures of that hand and get a copy of the emergency room report."

Matt asked, "Won't playing hardball make Meriah angrier?"

"Probably, but if there is a custody case, you want to make Meriah look as unstable as possible. I'm going to refer you to an experienced child custody lawyer. Here is her card. I suggest you contact her as soon as possible."

"If I could just talk to Meriah."

"Has she returned any of your calls?"

"No. I've texted, emailed, left messages on her phone, her publisher's, and her assistant's."

"I would suggest you keep a record of any and all attempts to contact Meriah."

"I will," assured Matt. "I'm worried Meriah has fallen ill, because it sounds like she's not in her right mind. You know, she didn't have an easy birth with Emmeline. It was very taxing for her."

"That is a possibility, and should be discussed with the custody lawyer. Maybe when you do get in touch with Meriah, you might suggest she see a doctor. Meriah might not even be aware that her behavior is frightening, but I feel you won't be able to speak to her for a very long time. The next person you hear from will be her lawyer." Shaneika leaned back in her high-backed leather chair. "And until the custody issue is resolved, I would recommend keeping your distance from Franklin."

"I don't know if I can do that. Franklin's my dear friend, and he's been like another parent to Emmeline."

"Precisely. Until Franklin is cleared of all charges, you should not have anything to do with him."

Matt looked aghast.

"But won't that hurt Franklin's credibility if his best friend shuns him?" I asked.

"Yes, it may," Shaneika replied coldly. "And that brings up another point. Either Franklin gets another lawyer, or both of you do. We have conflicting interests here."

Matt did not appear offended. "It's best Franklin stay with you. Whom shall we contact?"

"I've given you a good reference for a child custody lawyer. Josiah, if you need help with something, I recommend this lawyer." Shaneika handed me a different business card, which was the same as giving me my walking papers.

I took the card while snorting like an angry bull seeing red.

Things were becoming topsy-turvy and out of kilter.

I wanted clarity.

But most of all I wanted peace.

15

Asa followed Robin Russell into the discount store's parking lot.

Robin swirled around. "What do you want? I've already talked to you."

Asa held up her hands. "Whoa, there. What's wrong with answering a few more questions? You got something to hide?"

"Of course not, but you're not a real cop, and I've been interrogated several times by the police. I'm sick of being hounded."

"Maybe they think you're hiding something."

"I'm not," Robin said defiantly.

"I believe you, but I need some things cleared up."

"I don't know anything. Believe me, if I knew something, I would help. I like Franklin. I really do."

"I understand Franklin and Madison Smythe didn't get along."

"That's an understatement."

"Did Madison have problems with anyone else?"

"She got along with everyone."

"Really? Because other players said she was difficult," Asa lied.

Robin looked around the parking lot before speaking. "Well, if the others are saying things, then maybe I should, too." She leaned closer to Asa. "Madison was difficult. This group got together for fun and to put on a little play for our friends, but you'd think we were getting ready for Broadway. I mean, Madison was very demanding. It was ridiculous."

"How did that play out? No pun intended."

"At first we went along with her, but when it got so out of hand, several of the cast went to John and asked him to speak to Madison."

"Who was that?"

"Well, me. Then there were Zion Foley, Ashley Moore, and Deliah Webster."

"How did John react to complaints about his wife?"

"I don't know what he said to the others, but with me he said he would talk to her."

"How do you know the others went to talk to John?"

"They mentioned it in passing."

"And did he talk to Madison?"

"I don't know. John may have, but her behavior only got worse."

"What did the rest of the cast do?"

"Nothing. We were cowed. Only Franklin had the

guts to confront Madison."

"How many thespians are in this little group?"

Robin thought for a moment. "Let me see. Some-where between twelve and twenty. People drift in and out, according to their schedules."

Asa nodded slightly. This was similar to the number others had given her. "Why this particular play?"

"John suggested it. We had never done a murder mystery before, and it sounded like fun."

"What part did you play?"

"I played Madison's sister-in-law, Lady Elton."

Asa raised an eyebrow. "She's a Kentucky gal who marries an English lord."

"Yeah. That's right. How did you know?"

"Lucky guess. Now, were you in the scene where Madison drinks from the goblet?"

"Yes."

"Anyone else drink from the goblets?"

"Zion, who plays her lover."

"Did they always pick up the same goblet?"

"Yes. It's in the stage directions. The leading lady picks up the goblet on the left."

"Why is that?"

Robin shrugged. "Don't know. It's just in the stage directions."

"Do they pour from the wine decanter, or does the props manager fill the glasses beforehand?"

"Franklin always fills the goblets."

"Every time? Franklin says John filled up the goblets that night."

"He could have. I don't remember."

"Did Franklin fill the goblets every night?"

"Maybe not, but he's the props manager, so I just assumed he did."

"Why do you think Franklin disliked Madison so intensely?"

"Her attitude, for one thing."

Asa's ears perked up. "One thing? Was there another *thing*?"

Robin looked around the parking lot again. Was she searching for someone?

Asa did a quick scan too.

"Franklin told me earlier in the month he thought Madison was pinching things from Wickliffe Manor and asked me to keep an eye on her."

"Did you believe him?"

Robin shrugged. "I didn't want to get involved, but I told him I would."

"Did you keep an eye on Madison?"

"I told you. I didn't want to get involved in what was potentially messy, but I did see something."

Asa waited and waited until she said, "Well?"

"I saw John Smythe lift a carved jade trinket from an end table in the hallway and put it in Madison's coat pocket."

"Interesting."

"Yes, very."

"Did you tell Franklin it was John stealing and not Madison?"

"No."

"Because you didn't want to become involved," Asa interjected.

Robin looked uncomfortable. "I need to get going."

"Just give me a minute more. Do you think Franklin murdered Madison Smythe?"

Robin scoffed, "Franklin is the most gentle man I know. However, if a person was threatening someone whom Franklin loved, then yes, I can see Franklin killing him."

"You didn't answer my question."

"I don't think Franklin killed Madison. I don't even think Madison was murdered. She died of natural causes. This whole thing about arresting Franklin is a farce."

"The police think it was murder. They must have their reasons to think that."

Robin whinnied like a horse. Yes, she really did!

"One more question, please. Was Madison seeing someone on the side?"

Glancing away, Robin replied, "I wouldn't know, but if she was, ask Zion Foley. Now I've got to go." She opened her car door, was inside and gone before Asa could say Tippecanoe and Tyler too.

"I seem to have touched a nerve," Asa muttered to

herself before running to her car.

Why was Asa running?

She was going to follow Robin Russell.

16

Robin turned into a parking lot at Woodland Park in the Chevy Chase neighborhood. She got out of her car, scanned the street, and walked quickly into the park.

Asa pulled over on a side street, keeping Robin in her sights. She pulled her long hair under a hat and put on a sweater before grabbing a bag and quietly exiting her car. Making way to Robin's vehicle, she opened the locked door with some thingamajig from her bag. Keeping an eye on Robin walking toward the baseball field, Asa searched the car. It didn't take long. It was as clean as a whistle. Drats! Robin had taken her phone with her. Before locking the car back up, Asa put a listening and GPS tracking device under the dashboard.

Then Asa casually strolled down the sidewalk in the direction Robin had taken. Selecting a bench where she had a clear view, Asa sat and pulled knitting from her bag. Occasionally she looked through binoculars, as though birdwatching as well.

After waiting about ten minutes, a young man in his

early twenties ambled from High Street into the park. He carried sacks of what looked like takeout lunch.

Robin ran up to him, and they hugged each other tightly.

"Well, the game is afoot, Watson," Asa quoted to no one in particular. Like her mother, Asa had a fondness for Sherlock Homes. She twisted her mouth in frustration. She knew Robin was married with one child and in her early thirties. So who was this young guy, and what was he to Robin? Hmm.

Robin and the young man sat on a bench facing away from Asa and began eating their lunch. Frequently, Robin would lean over and kiss the young man on the cheek.

Asa decided to get closer so she could hear the conversation. She strolled casually behind their bench, catching snippets and heard Robin call the young man Ashley while discussing his college work.

Moving behind a tree, Asa fished for a camera and took pictures of the couple.

When they finished their lunch, they bagged it up and threw it in a trash container. Robin gave the young man money, and the two parted ways.

Asa decided to follow Ashley. She tracked him to an old, rundown Toyota. He pulled out of his parking spot like a bat out of hell, but not before Asa memorized his license plate.

Leaning against a ginkgo tree and watching the car

speed down High Street, Asa wondered if the young man was the Ashley Moore who also acted in the play. And better yet, why was Robin Russell meeting him for lunch in a park and giving him money?

Inquiring minds wanted to know.

Asa's inquiring mind, to be exact.

17

It didn't take Asa long to track Ashley down. He lived in a downtown apartment near the University of Kentucky with two roommates.

Asa watched the comings and goings from Ashley's apartment for several hours. There was so much foot traffic, Asa was beginning to wonder if Ashley and his roommates were selling drugs.

Suddenly two boys, one of them Ashley, and a girl, exited the apartment and walked past Asa's car, probably going to dinner.

Asa saw this as an opportunity to snoop and took it. The lock was weak, so Asa used a credit card to get in.

It was a typical college apartment. Dirty dishes in the sink, clothes draped over chairs, and empty beer bottles tossed on the makeshift coffee table, but no evidence of drugs.

Asa checked the bedrooms. The first one belonged to a female. A bra hung over a chair while an open makeup bag and a basket of clean laundry lay on the bed, a biology textbook opened on the desk next to a computer—typical college girl room.

Asa moved on to the next bedroom. It was a pigsty. Beer bottles strewn on the floor. Clothes scattered everywhere. Unmade bed. Asa picked up a pair of jeans off the floor. Too big for Ashley. This must be his roommate's bedroom.

She tried the door to the last bedroom. It was locked. No problem. Asa slipped her credit card in the lock. Voila!

Asa stepped inside one of the cleanest bedrooms she had ever been in. "Someone has OCD," she muttered, picking up a silver frame. It contained a picture of Ashley with two older individuals whom Asa surmised were his parents. Asa put the frame back on the dresser. She moved to the desk where she whispered, "Uh oh," when she saw a wallet.

Ashley had forgotten his money.

Asa moved to leave the apartment when a shadow fell across the threshold. She looked up and saw Ashley between her and escape.

"Who are you?" demanded Ashley, looking somewhat confused and a little afraid.

Since Ashley was tall and muscular, Asa was thinking of ways to knock him unconscious, but would prefer to get out of the apartment on her own steam and not hurt the kid.

"I'm Mary Sharp. I live in 4B. I was about to leave

when I noticed your front door was open."

"It was?" Ashley narrowed his eyes. "Okay, but what are you doing in my bedroom? I lock it when I go out."

"Is this your bedroom? Oh my goodness!" exclaimed "Mary" while moving toward Ashley as he took a step back into the hallway. "I called out to let someone know the front door wasn't closed properly, and when I didn't hear anyone, I came in to check. To make sure no one was hurt, you know."

Mary brushed by Ashley into the living room. "You can't be too careful. I watch all those crime shows, and I wanted to make sure no one was injured or dead. Do you watch any of those shows?"

"Sometimes."

"You know what I'm talking about, then?"

"I guess so."

"Looks like everyone is okay, and seems the front door was left open by mistake. You should be thankful that it was me passing by, and not some opportunist thief. That's a blessing, isn't it? Well, I've got to go. I'm having dinner with my boyfriend, and I'm late. See ya later."

Asa gave one last wave and bounded down the wooden apartment steps.

Ashley followed her out and watched her, giving a feeble wave.

Out of the corner of her eye, she saw him head for

apartment 4B, but by the time he would find out "Mary" didn't live there, Asa would be long gone.

That was a close call.

Asa thought she must be losing her touch, allowing herself to be discovered by a college boy.

She'd been caught snooping twice in one week—once in Hunter's house and now in Ashley's apartment.

This was not a good thing in her line of business.

Not good at all.

18

I got stuck with Emmeline again, but I still had to repair and paint my pasture fences, so I gathered up the baby and my Baby, along with Ginger.

Malcolm, one of Charles' grandsons, met me in the front pasture by the road and helped me lift the pop-up playpen out of my golf cart. Baby jumped out and tried to get into it. I shooed him away and unbuckled the baby from her car seat, put her in one of those bouncy/learn playgrounds toymakers make for babies nowadays, and sat it in the middle of the playpen. "Baby. Ginger. Guard," I ordered.

Baby sneezed and meekly lay down by the playpen, putting his massive head on his front paws. Within moments, he was lying on his side snoring. Ginger sat beside the playpen alert, taking her guarding duties far more seriously.

Emmeline jumped up and down happily in her bouncy seat, gurgling. As long as she could see me, the baby was content.

"Where are we?" I asked Malcolm.

"All the repairs to the two front pastures are done. I finished this morning. We can paint anytime you want."

"Do you have the paint sprayers ready?"

"All I've got to do is get them out of my truck and pour in the paint."

"Okay, let's do it. I'll take this pasture so I can keep an eye on the baby."

Malcolm frowned. "Won't the paint blow on the kid?"

"Don't worry, Malcolm. I have raised a child of my own, and I used to babysit you, remember?"

Malcolm rubbed his backside. "I sure do."

I gave him a playful punch on his shoulder. "You know I never gave you a spanking. I just ratted you out to your grandfather when you were bad."

"That was enough to keep me in line," said Malcolm, grinning.

"It was like money in the bank to get you to behave."

Malcolm chuckled while he pulled out the paint sprayers and poured paint into their buckets.

My horse fences were common to the area—six-inch, round oak posts about eight feet apart attached to four sixteen-foot-long horizontal planks. Here's another little tidbit I bet you didn't know . . . all horse fences have to be rounded at the corners. There are no right-angle fences where horses are concerned, since they like to run along the fence line. They must have fences that curve so they won't run into them.

Also, pastures where stallions are kept must have double rows of fences to keep them apart. Stallions are not friendly with one another.

When I was growing up, all farms painted their fences white, but that had died out due to the high cost of repainting them every two years. If you didn't keep the fences looking pristine, folks knew you had fallen on hard times. Nowadays, most horse fences are painted black with creosote paint because it requires less upkeep and expense.

I was a couple of years overdue for painting my fences. They were looking kind of ratty, but then I *had* fallen on hard times.

The pasture I was painting used to be home to Comanche. There was a doubled-rowed fence in the front to keep people from the road having any contact with him, and doubled-rowed fence in the back to keep him from having any contact with other horses.

Comanche's current pasture was closer to the Butterfly, since he was now very valuable. Horse rustling is not unheard of in the Bluegrass.

I didn't care for Comanche. He always tried to bite me. The only people he cared for were Shaneika, her son Linc, and his trainer. Even jockeys didn't like him. He was too ornery, but Shaneika was now winning races with him.

Shaneika was doing the unthinkable. Most horse people make their money from the breeding fees. That's where the money is. They don't let their champions race after a few years, because they could be injured and limit their ability to "cover" a mare.

But Shaneika didn't care about that. She wanted a champion that would go down in legend like Man o' War, Seabiscuit, or War Admiral.

Personally, I didn't think Comanche had it in him to become the racehorse of Shaneika's dream, but he was winning important stake races. I had to admit Shaneika had done a superb job with him, especially after his disastrous first race where he came in dead last.

But she charged ahead with him, and Comanche lost the Kentucky Derby by a nose. A nose! The defeat was hard for Shaneika to swallow, but she rebounded, as did Comanche. Since then he had been on a lightning streak, winning ninety percent of all races Shaneika entered him in.

At the moment, I didn't have to bother with him, because Comanche was training at Keeneland. I used this opportunity to remove any muck from the fields, repair the fences, and clean his stall until it shone like a star from heaven.

I was about finished painting the first row of fence line along the road when I began picking up trash. It disgusted me that people threw their drink cups and fast food sacks alongside the road. The litter cluttered the countryside, was filthy to look at, and could injure animals that might be attracted. I just don't understand people who throw garbage out of their cars. I really don't.

Are they jealous? Do they have contempt for the area in which they live? Are they tourists? If they do this to the beautiful countryside, what do their houses look like?

Enough of my rant. Emmeline was crying.

Baby sat up and whined, looking at me as if to say, "Hey, the kid's upset. Do something!"

A quick diaper change didn't stop the crying. Okay. I know you're not to coddle crying babies, but I hate it when they cry, so I made a makeshift baby sling across my back, which seem to do the trick, but the baby was heavy and slowed me down. I had only painted a fourth of what Malcolm had painted on the other pasture fence when I had to stop.

Malcolm came over. "What's wrong?"

"What's wrong? I can't paint with a baby on my back, and I'm too damned old to be doing this. That's what's wrong."

"Your face is awfully red."

"Great. Now I'm gonna have a heart attack to boot."

"I'll get one of my brothers to help me."

"I can't afford it, Malcolm."

"Shoot! With all the money you're making?"

"Sometime soon, you need to have your grandfather show you Lady Elsmere's books so you can learn how much it costs to operate a horse farm in the Bluegrass. Money comes in, but honey, it sure goes out again in a hurry to pay the bills."

Malcolm seemed bored with my lecture. "How do you want to handle this?"

"It's almost lunchtime. I'm going to feed the baby, and then put her down for her nap. I'll bring back the baby monitor with me and maybe get in a couple hours of work before she wakes up."

Malcolm gave me a sideways look which said, "You can't cut the mustard anymore, old lady."

I didn't argue, because Malcolm was right.

And I proved him right. After I put Emmeline down, I checked to make sure the house was secure before I left to finish the fence. Emmeline was fussing, so I thought I would lie down in the room until she fell asleep. *Just for a few minutes,* I thought to myself.

Just a few minutes.

19

I awoke. I guess from snoring and drooling. Charming. Oh, gosh! It was late afternoon. I sat straight up. Emmeline!

She was fine. Another diaper fix. A bottle. Change her clothes. Time to get back to work.

By the time I reached the front pasture, Malcolm was still spraying creosote paint on the fences. I put Emmeline in the bouncy seat and left Baby to guard her.

"You okay?"

"Yeah," I said, picking up a sprayer. "I've forgotten how much work it is to take care of a baby."

"If you say so."

"I do say so, and if you're not careful with the ladies, you'll be saying it, too."

Malcolm grinned. "You think I'm a ladies' man?"

"I see you driving around with that souped-up muscle car of yours. Those cars attract the *laa-dees*."

"I got no time for them. Keeping my head down

and studying. I want to help Grandpa when he inherits Lady Elsmere's estate. I'm gonna take animal husbandry and economics at college. Take lots of pre-vet courses."

"Want to be one of the big boys in the horse racing business, do ya?"

"I'm more interested in the breeding aspect of it. I want to breed champions. Another Secretariat. Another Affirmed."

"Those kinds of horses are few and far between. Both of them had enormous lung capacity."

"I want to establish another racing record like Calumet Farm. My brothers are interested in racing, and I'm interested in providing the fastest horses possible. It's a win-win."

"That's a big dream, Malcolm."

"You think I'm wrong?"

"I think a young man should have a big dream and go after it. Don't let anyone stop you, Malcolm. Not anyone."

"You're all right, Miss Josiah."

"Let's get some work done, buddy boy. The sun won't wait on us."

We worked several more hours, with Malcolm taking the lead. Luckily, we got the last section painted before Emmeline began fussing.

I looked at my watch. Matt would be home soon, and he could take over. I had a little time left to clean up, make a fast dinner, and fall into bed.

As we were heading home, I sang *Itsy Bitsy Spider* to Emmeline while planning dinner—something quick and easy.

Huh! That's what I thought. Boy, was I stupid!

20

Matt and Asa arrived home about the same time. As soon as Matt set down his briefcase, I handed him Emmeline. I was done for the day.

And before Asa could open her mouth, I gave her a list of ingredients to get from the pantry and instructed her to boil some eggs.

I took a shower, washing the paint out of my hair, and dressed in clean clothes. After brushing my wet hair, I felt human again and ventured into the kitchen.

Asa had boiled the eggs and set my Nakashima table. I made some tuna salad, a quick spring lettuce salad, and sliced some fresh tomatoes. It was salad, salad, salad all the way. Something quick and fast to make, but I have to say my tuna salad is very good. Asa pulled hot yeast rolls out of the oven.

We sat down to dinner. I could tell we were all worn out from the day, and it didn't help that Emmeline was fussy. She certainly didn't like the orange gruel Matt was trying to shove into her mouth. Most of it was on

Emmeline's face while Matt pleaded with her.

I've got to tell you, at that moment I understood why crocodiles ate their young.

"Matt, put her on the floor," I suggested.

"That filthy floor where Baby has slobbered?"

"Believe me, a few germs here and there will only boost Emmeline's immune system."

Asa piped up, "Yeah, Mom used to take me to the riverbank and roll me in the mud."

Matt stared at her for a moment. "You're kidding, right?"

"Matt, I swear that bullet made you dim-witted," said Asa before stuffing a roll into her mouth.

"How was today's sleuthing?" I asked Asa.

"People are lying through their teeth, and I don't know why. Do you know of any relationship between Ashley Moore and Robin Russell?"

"What do you mean?"

"Is there a special thing between them?"

"You mean romantically? She's almost old enough to be his mother."

"I saw them having lunch together in Woodland Park this afternoon. She was fondling him, and then she gave Ashley a nice little wad of money."

"Define fondling," Matt said, watching Baby sniff Emmeline.

Asa thought for a moment. "Caressing his hair. Touching his shoulder. Hugging him. That kind of thing."

Matt replied, "That could mean any number of things. Depends on one's interpretation."

"I've only known them to be professional with each other at the rehearsals. I haven't noticed anything untoward."

"Something's going on between them, but that's just part of this. Everyone is saying how fantastic Madison was to work with, and how they loved her."

"What do they say about Franklin?"

"They are very fond of him and grateful to his brother for the use of Wickliffe Manor."

"I have no idea what's going on," I replied before salting my tomatoes. "It's a mystery."

"Yuck. Yuck," snarked Asa.

The doorbell rang.

Matt asked, "Who can that be?"

"I changed the codes again. Nobody but people at the Big House and Shaneika have the new numbers."

"What about the other horse boarders?" Asa asked.

"I haven't told them about the code change yet. Nobody is due. Malcolm and Juan take care of the horses now."

Asa wiped her mouth before folding her napkin. "Let me have a look-see." Baby followed her to the front door.

Matt picked up Emmeline and took her into the guest bedroom, locking the door behind him.

Since Meriah's visit, everyone was on edge.

I heard Asa open the front door and talk to some-one. When she came back, Hunter followed her into the great room. Baby remained in the foyer. We could hear someone talking to him. Then Baby bounded into the great room followed by Franklin. He looked pale and thin.

"Franklin!" I was surprised but happy to see him. "They let you out of Sing Sing."

Franklin gave me a peck on the cheek and sat down at the dining table. "I see we are in time for dinner."

"Of course," I replied, rushing to set two more places at the table.

"I'll do it, Mom," Asa offered. "You relax."

I sat next to Franklin while Hunter sat on the oppo-site side of the table, beaming at his baby brother.

"Well, give us the details," I demanded.

"Hunter sold his Rolls to get me out of jail."

I looked at Hunter to gauge his reaction. I knew how much he loved his beat-up Rolls.

"It was the only thing of value I could sell. I had no idea nobody wanted sterling silver tea sets anymore. They are valuable only to dowagers who still use them and insurance companies who want to insure them."

"You couldn't get a credit line on Wickliffe Man-or?" I asked.

"I can get another mortgage on the farm, but that's to pay for Franklin's legal fees. It's one thing at a time with this."

Asa set the table and poured wine into their glasses. "Let's hope it doesn't come to that. I'm making some interesting headway."

Franklin asked, "What do you mean?"

"Everyone is lying, and I mean everyone. I don't understand why, but I'm close to proving someone was setting your brother up as a romantic lead for Madison."

Asa directed her gaze at Hunter. "I took the liberty of having your handwriting and that of the love note analyzed by a professional. She says the love note is not your handwriting and can prove it in a court of law."

"I told you I didn't write it."

"And now I believe you. Tuna salad?"

"Why would anyone try to frame me? I didn't even know those people." Hunter looked at us as though expecting an answer, but we had no idea.

Franklin handed his plate to Asa. "I'll take some tuna, please. Josiah, can you hand me the garden salad and dressing?"

"Sure," I replied, handing him a bowl. "What's next?"

Hunter answered, "I've got a couple of consulting cases out of town, so I would appreciate it, Asa, if you would continue your investigation. I'll pay you somehow."

"This is pro bono, but I have to leave next week. I better find something by then."

"What?" I said. "I thought you would stay longer."

"Mom, believe it or not, I have a business to run and a living to make. Franklin, I'm sorry, but there it is. After I leave, Shaneika's PI, Walter Neff, will take over."

Everyone groaned in unison.

Franklin wiped his mouth with a linen napkin. "No problem, Asa. I appreciate what you've done so far."

"Think nothing of it, kiddo."

Hunter and I traded glances but said nothing.

Franklin scanned the great room while stuffing his mouth and noticed all the baby toys. "We stopped at Matt's house, but no one was home. Do you know where he is?"

Here was the question I had been dreading. "While you were in jail, Meriah created quite a ruckus about Emmeline."

"Oh? Is that why your pinky is trussed up in that metal thingamajig?"

"Frankly, yes. She came to the Butterfly and demanded to take Emmeline. She even had a cop with her."

Hunter asked, "What happened?"

"We had a tussle, and she broke my finger."

Franklin sputtered, "You—you had a girl fight with Meriah?" He laughed. "I would have paid a king's ransom to witness that."

"Franklin, hush. It isn't funny," Hunter chided.

"Look at Josiah's expression."

"Sorry, but the thought of it tickles my funny bone. Please tell me you whomped Meriah upside the head, but good."

"No, Franklin. It isn't funny. In fact, I'm in a huge custody battle with Meriah now," came a voice from the hall.

We all turned to see Matt enter the great room.

Franklin jumped up and ran over to hug Matt, but Matt kept him at arm's length. "I need to talk to you, Franklin, about a serious matter."

"You mean more serious than my being arrested for murder?"

"Equally important, and a life-changing event."

"Okay, so talk."

"Let's go outside and talk in private."

Franklin stared into Matt's face. "I don't like your expression. It says 'I'm about to screw you over, Franklin.'"

"Meriah has sued for custody of Emmeline."

"Why now? She hasn't seemed very interested in *our* baby before."

"Emmeline isn't our baby. She's *my* baby."

Franklin gasped and stepped away from Matt.

Hunter stood up and threw his napkin on the table, but I reached over and grabbed his hand.

"Don't," I cautioned. "Let them duke it out. This has been coming on for a long time." I could see the veins in Franklin's neck throbbing. This was not going to be pretty.

"How can you say that? I spend more time with her than you. I feed her, change her, clothe her, burp her, worry over her, read to her, take her to the doctor. I am as much a parent to her as you are."

"I know, Franklin, but I am fighting for legal rights to my child, and right now, you are an . . . an entanglement I can't afford. You have been arrested for first-degree murder—a capital offense. That's not going to look good before a judge."

Franklin staggered away and fell into a chair.

I declared, "Matt, you're saying things you are going to regret and can't take back."

Matt warned, "Stay out of this, Josiah. This is not your battle."

Franklin accused, "You mean I'm an embarrassment, don't you? I was framed for a murder through no fault of my own, and this makes me an embarrassment. Where's the support, Matt?"

"I've been advised by my custody lawyer that you pose a threat to keeping Emmeline."

"I . . . I pose a threat?" Franklin repeated the words, seemingly dumbfounded. "Are you cutting me out of your life for good?"

Matt didn't answer. I could see his jaw muscles clench.

"I think you want to get rid of me, and you're using

this custody suit to do it," Franklin argued.

"That does it," Hunter groused. "Matt, you have done nothing but make my brother's life miserable ever since he met you. I have no idea what he sees in you."

"Hunter, don't. You'll only make things worse," I said, trying to put a plug in this conversation. Everyone needed to cool off. "Why don't we all take a deep breath, resume dinner, and talk about this after dessert."

Matt sneered, "Here comes the big brother routine. Where were you when Franklin was shot, Hunter? Nowhere, man. He said you called a couple of times and that was it. Where was your brotherly concern then? I'm the one who took care of Franklin—and Josiah, too. I paid for much of Franklin's medical bills. You didn't even bother to ask Franklin if he had health insurance to cover all his expenses. It was a bad scene, but you were in London, having a great time."

"I was going through a nasty divorce."

"You told me your ex-wives were friendly," I blurted.

Hunter answered, "They are very friendly now they have all my money."

Asa shouted, "EVERYONE SHUT UP! This is getting out of hand. Franklin, Hunter, Matt. Sit down and finish your dinner. All of you are stressed out and tired. Come on, now. This is no way to act."

Matt immediately turned and stormed back to his room.

Franklin sat motionless, shocked, his mouth gaping open, making him look like a hooked fish gasping for air.

Hunter grabbed Franklin's arm and hauled him up from the chair. "Let's go, Franklin. There's nothing for us here."

"Wait a minute," I snapped. "That's not true."

"Do you agree with Matt?" Franklin asked me.

"No, Franklin, I don't, but I do understand his fear of losing his daughter. That type of fear makes parents do irrational things. Please, please, don't go like this."

"I HATE YOU, MATTHEW GARTH! I HATE YOU! DO YOU HEAR ME?" screamed Franklin as Hunter dragged him out of the Butterfly. Hunter slammed the front door.

"Jumping Jehosaphat! I need a stiff drink," I said, holding my stomach. It felt like I had a ton of rocks churning in my gut.

Asa sat down and resumed eating dinner. In between bites, she mumbled, "Well, that was certainly dinner and a show."

I plopped down beside her and put my head in my hands. "Matt is unkind to Franklin. He's always been a flirt and a philanderer, but he's never been bone mean to anyone, except to Franklin. And I've never understood it, because I know Matt loves him."

"Man kills the thing he loves."

"Stop being flippant, Asa. This is very serious."

"I am serious." Asa paused, deep in thought before speaking again. "Very serious, and I think I just solved the case. All I need is proof."

"Really?"

"Yes, but right now, I'm going to have a bowl of blackberry cobbler with ice cream and go to bed. What time will you be up in the morning?"

"Early. Eunice is coming to go over some bookings at the Butterfly."

"I will brief you then, but I have a little chore for you to do tomorrow."

"Can't you tell me now?"

Asa rubbed her hands together and cackled like the Wicked Witch of the West in *The Wizard of Oz.* "All in good time, my pretty. All in good time."

21

"GO AWAY!"

You know me. I opened the door and strode in.

Matt was standing over the crib, watching Emmeline sleep.

"You want to talk?"

"No."

"Too bad. I have a few things to say."

Matt snarled, "I don't want to hear them."

"Matt, you've got to forgive yourself."

Startled, Matt glared at me. "What for?"

"You've always felt guilty about what happened to Franklin, Baby, and me. There was nothing you could have done to prevent what happened. In fact, you would have gotten yourself killed."

Tears spilled out of Matt's eyes and streaked down his cheek. "If I hadn't taken so long to park the car that night, I could have stopped him."

We both purposely didn't mention the perpetrator's name, but you know of whom we spoke.

"No, you couldn't have. He would have taken you out first, because you were the strongest. Since that night, you have behaved like a jerk toward Franklin."

"We've had this conversation before."

"And you still haven't straightened out."

"I can't be what he wants me to be."

"Which is?"

"Monogamous, for starters."

"Ever use self-control for once? Heterosexuals have those urges, too, but if we love our mates, we try to steer clear of affairs. Some of us even manage to do so. Sooner or later, your looks are going to fade. Offers will be fewer and fewer. I'll be dead by that time, of course. You will have chased Emmeline off due to your embarrassing sexual escapades with her 'uncles,' and you'll end up all alone."

"That's my future?"

"Pretty much, at the rate you're going, or you can sow seeds for a happy future. Sacrifice is a handy word you might try wrapping your mind around."

"Are you saying I should stay with Franklin?"

"I'm saying that whatever you decide, quit being cruel. If you are going to cut Franklin out, use a sharp, clean knife. Quit calling him when you need help or feel lonely. He's a good man. He deserves a better friend than you."

"Ouch. That hurts, Josiah."

"Real friends tell the truth."

"Are you still my friend?"

"George Bailey, I'll love you till the day I die," I quoted from *It's A Wonderful Life*, one of my favorite movies before reaching out to Matt.

We held hands as we stood gazing at Emmeline sleeping the sleep of the innocent.

22

I knocked on Robin's door.

She opened it and upon seeing me, made a face. "What do you want?"

I stuck my foot in the opening in case she tried to slam the door in my face. I hoped she wouldn't do it though, since it would hurt my footsies. "Robin, we need to talk."

Robin let out a loud sigh. "NO! I'm sick of you people."

I held up a photo of her with Ashley.

She grabbed it, tore it up, and threw the fragments at me, looking triumphant.

"I've got six more pictures of you at Woodland Park with Ashley, and Asa has the images backed up on a remote server. Please, we need to talk."

"Asa," Robin spat out. "She's such a b . . ."

"Ah, ah, ah, let's be civil. You don't want to make me mad."

Realizing she was going to have to give up her secrets, Robin let me in, and I followed her into the living room.

She sat on the couch, and I sat in an adjacent chair—an uncomfortable chair, at that.

She lit a cigarette and blew smoke in my direction. Cute.

"Robin, I wouldn't be so insistent, but everyone is lying, including you, about the night Madison died. Franklin is in real trouble. You know he didn't kill Madison. What's up with you?"

Robin looked away and muttered, "I'm afraid. That's why."

I was stunned. "Afraid of what?"

"I'm afraid of the real murderer."

"But why?"

"Because I know how Madison died."

"The ME's report hasn't been released yet."

"I'm telling you, I know what killed Madison."

"I'm all ears," I encouraged, leaning forward.

"She died of cyanide poisoning, like the heroine in the play."

"Why do you say that?"

"Because I smelled burnt almonds. That's what cyanide smells like." She put out her cigarette and then lit another one. "You didn't get close to the body. I did. When I put a blanket on Madison, I leaned over her face. That's when I smelled it. Her breath stank."

"But Franklin and Hunter were close to the body,

and they never mentioned smelling anything odd."

"They are brothers, and the ability to smell cyanide is a genetic trait. Forty percent of the people there that night would not have been able to detect it."

"But why didn't you tell the police?"

"Because I shrieked when I smelled it, and I'm sure the murderer heard me. I wasn't able to mask my surprise at my discovery, and now I'm afraid I'll be next."

"If it was cyanide, it will be in the ME's report. You smelling it wouldn't put you in danger. It was bound to come out."

I was skeptical of Robin's story. Cyanide is hard to come by anymore unless you find an old bottle of rat poison, and I didn't remember Robin shrieking. "You must have seen something else of importance, Robin? What was it?"

"I saw John place the goblets on the table."

"Why does that concern you?"

"That was Franklin's job. I had never seen John handle the props before."

"So you think John poisoned Madison?"

"Yes."

"Why?"

"Ask Zion. That's all I'll say on the matter."

"Okay, let's get back to Ashley. Why did you give him money?"

"He needed some money, so I floated him a friendly loan."

"Come on, now. Asa said you couldn't keep your hands off him."

"Asa had no business following me. I should go to the police about her."

"If you do, I'll show these pictures to your husband." Rest assured I can get down and dirty if someone I love is threatened. Oh, yes, I can.

Robin blanched. "Please don't. It would make trouble for me."

"Tell me the truth."

Robin thought for a moment while chewing on another cigarette. "He's my son."

"What?"

"I'm telling the truth. I had him when I was fifteen and put him up for adoption. He came to school in Lexington so he could track me down."

"And?"

"I was caught off guard, but once I got over the shock, I was happy to see him. He's grown into such a handsome man, like his father. It certainly has taken a terrible burden off my shoulders to know my son is doing fine."

"How did he find out about you? Aren't adoption records supposed to be sealed?"

"A distant relative of my father's adopted him. That man died, and when Ashley was going through his papers, he found a letter about me. He knew he was adopted, but he didn't know who his birth mother was until then."

"Ashley's father?"

"Oh, my gosh, I hadn't thought of him in years. He was a teenage crush that got out of hand. I don't even know where Ashley's father lives. I haven't heard from him since Ashley was born."

"I take it that your family doesn't know about him."

"Not even my husband."

"But why keep it a secret?"

"Because of Ashley's behavior. I have to be sure of Ashley before I introduce him to my family."

"What does that mean?"

"He didn't come up and introduce himself to me. Ashley tracked me down and must have spied on me, because he joined our drama group without telling me who he was. I had no idea.

"After a few months, he told me who he was while we were standing in the driveway of Wickliffe Manor. I was stunned. He knew where I lived, where I worked, and who my friends were. It creeped me out. I mean, don't get me wrong. I was thrilled, but part of me chilled at the thought that he was stalking me. Before I turn my husband and child's lives upside down, I have to be sure about Ashley. That's why this murder is so inconvenient. It may force me to confess about Ashley before I'm ready."

"I'm sure Madison's family will feel your pain."

"Oh, don't be so righteous. You know what I mean."

"Do you think Ashley has anything to do with Madison's death?"

"I have said this over and over. I don't think Madison was killed. I think she died of natural causes."

"You just said a few moments ago you thought John had poisoned Madison with cyanide."

"Did I?" Robin asked, seemingly confused.

"You said you smelled something on her breath."

"How could I smell something on her breath if she was dead?"

"Before she died, Robin. When she went into convulsions. You said you put a blanket on her."

"No, I never said that. Zion put a blanket on her, and that was after Hunter put her back on the couch."

I looked into Robin's eyes. She didn't have the look of deceit in them. There was something going on here that wasn't kosher.

"I won't tell anyone about your relationship with Ashley, except for Franklin's lawyer."

Robin inhaled deeply from her cigarette, exhaled, and crushed the remainder in an ashtray. "Thank you. I need some breathing room to deal with Ashley. Sorry I couldn't have been more help."

Getting up to leave, I said, "I'll see myself out." Leaving the room, I glanced back to see Robin light up another cigarette. I made up my mind to call Robin's husband and suggest she see a doctor. My guess was she'd had a stroke, but Robin was so young.

I hoped I was wrong, but something wasn't right.

23

I knew where Zion Foley had lunch every day, so I decided that I would "casually" run into him. I walked into Stella's Deli, ordered at the counter, paid, and looked around for a table to sit at. There was Zion, sitting in the corner by himself, eating a banana and peanut butter sandwich.

"Zion, can I join you? The other tables are taken."

Zion looked up from his newspaper and smiled. "Well, Josiah. Fancy meeting you here. This isn't your usual stomping ground."

I have to confess my heart fluttered a little bit. Zion was a handsome man, and when he smiled, the sun came out. Black hair, pale blue eyes, and dimples.

"May I?"

"Sure. Let me move my things off the seat." He moved an opened briefcase onto the floor.

"Thank you," I said, sitting down.

A clerk called my name.

"I'll get it," Zion offered.

"That's very sweet of you."

As soon as Zion's back was turned, I leaned over and rifled through his briefcase. I pulled up just in the nick of time.

Zion put my chicken salad sandwich and hot tea on the table, along with several napkins. "What brings you to this part of town?"

"I had a dental appointment."

"Really? I didn't know there were any medical offices in this area."

"She's new. Yep, she's new," I babbled, bobbing my head like a doll on a car dashboard. "But I'm glad I ran into you. Franklin's out on bail."

"Really? How's he doing?"

"Not too well, Zion. Not too well."

"Really? That's too bad. I think the police are batty, you know?"

I wished he'd quit saying "really." He sounded like a wind-up toy. "Why do you say that?"

"I don't know if Madison was murdered or not, but if she was, the obvious place to look would be in John's direction." Zion's eyes got a little weepy.

"Really?" Oh, good Lord. Now I was saying it.

"He was awful to Madison. Didn't love her, just used her as a bank account," Zion said heatedly.

I must have had a surprised look on my face because Zion's face turned red.

"Sorry. I think this affair has all of us in the drama

club upset."

He used the word "affair," not I, so I decided to take a chance.

I reached out and patted his hand. "I know how much Madison meant to you. This must be especially hard for you."

Zion pulled back. "What do you mean, Jo?"

"You don't need to deny it with me. We all knew about it. None of us judged you."

"Judged me?" Zion reared back in his chair. Oh dear, the dimples were gone. "Judged me for what?"

"Well, you know. Madison and you."

Zion looked surprised, then angry, and finally resigned. He took a sip of his sweet tea—the official wine of the South.

"Do you think John knew?" Now, my figuring of the situation was either Zion would deny an affair, storm off appalled, and never to speak to me again, or he would relent and, feeling guilty, confess. I waited quietly. Sometimes it pays to be quiet. As they say, the next one who speaks loses the game.

"Did Madison tell you about us?"

BINGO! What did I tell you?

Ignoring his question, I asked one of my own. "Do the police know?"

"Yes. I told them."

"Why?"

"I was afraid Madison hadn't kept quiet about us,

and people knew—as you said. I didn't want to get on the cops' radar for lying. You know how she was."

I nodded, wondering where this was going.

"Impulsive. Mercurial."

"Was Madison going to leave John?"

"She had the money in the marriage, and was afraid she would have to give John a sizable chunk of it if they did divorce."

"No prenup, huh?"

"Yes, there was, but John would have tied Madison up in court for months or even years trying to break it because she was the one cheating. She didn't want to waste money on lawyers, so she stayed and endured. She thought sooner or later, John would grow tired of the situation. Madison always said as long as she had me, she was content to stay in the marriage until John drifted away."

"And that was okay with you?"

"For the time being." Zion shifted uncomfortably in his seat. "I've been in love before, and realize that it can fade. I was waiting to see if this relationship would last."

"An affair is a pretty tough way to test love, Zion."

"You're telling me." He grinned, and the dimples were back.

"Some cast members have said Madison might have stolen valuables from Wickliffe Manor. Do you think Madison was stealing from Hunter?"

"Naw. She was grateful to Hunter for letting us use his house."

I took a bite of my sandwich. "Then why do you think Franklin accused Madison of stealing?"

"I've never understood it."

"Did Madison have a habit of taking little things if she was upset? Sometimes that's how people deal with stress."

"Not that I'm aware of." Zion fiddled with his fork.

Oops, my internal lie detector went off. The little pen was zigzagging off the paper. "Did you ever leave love notes in her coat pocket?"

Zion started laughing. "What is this—the third degree? Did you *just* happen to run into me?"

"I'm so sorry, Zion. I get carried away. You know how I love mysteries."

"It's not a game, Josiah. Someone I cared for deeply has died," Zion said, grimacing.

I bowed my head. For a brief moment I was ashamed, but it passed. "You are so right. Let's talk about something else. How 'bout them Cats?" I said, referring to the University Of Kentucky's basketball program.

Zion angrily tossed some bills on the table and stormed out of the deli.

"He must really be upset with me," I murmured to myself.

The woman at the next table leaned over and asked,

"What's that?"

"Nothing," I replied, smiling.

"Would you be a dear and move your briefcase off the floor? I almost tripped over it."

I looked down at Zion's briefcase next to my feet. "There is a god," I muttered as I scooped up the briefcase. "Oh, I dropped it, and everything has spilled out. How clumsy of me. Give me a minute, ma'am, while I'll put everything back, and get it out of your way."

"I would appreciate it," she said, giving me a look that proclaimed I was a complete imbecile.

I didn't mind being thought of as stupid while picking up each letter and scrap of paper and scanning it before stuffing it in the briefcase. I had to hurry. It would only be a matter of minutes before Zion realized his mistake and stomped back to retrieve the briefcase.

I hummed happily as I went through Zion's papers. A busybody doesn't encounter a windfall like this every day. Sometimes I amaze myself at my deviousness, but the trait can come in handy. It was certainly paying off at the moment.

24

Deliah Webster was one of those perpetually cheerful people who was very attractive. She was also very dull-witted. She irritated both friends and strangers alike by saying things like "Let's turn that frown upside down" or "This is the most important second of your life. Live to the fullest."

Didn't matter if people had terminal cancer or just lost a spouse to divorce, Deliah would try to cheer them up with one of her upbeat quotes, as if their lives weren't in shambles enough without listening to her prattle. All they had to do was smile, according to Deliah, and the feeling of utter abandonment and bereavement would magically evaporate.

Deliah worked at a store in Fayette Mall where she demonstrated expensive cookware.

Asa was watching her through the store window the way a cougar watches a fat, juicy rabbit nibbling on clover. She could barely stop licking her chops before flouncing into the store.

"May I help you?" Deliah asked. She was wearing a low-cut blouse to show off some of her best assets.

Asa replied in a high-pitched New Jersey accent, "I'm looking for some cookware. I just moved into a new house, and I want everything to be perfect."

"I understand."

"Nothing with copper on the base. I don't want to spend my time polishing and buffing . . . but beautiful, you know?"

"I was just going to suggest our new copper pans."

Asa scrunched up her nose.

"They are not copper on the bottom, but inside the pans, and they're non-stick. They clean very easily."

Asa popped a piece of gum into her mouth. "I don't care. I won't be doing the dishes. That's the maid's job." She elbowed Deliah and laughed.

"You just moved to Lexington?"

"Yeah, my husband bought a horse farm and redid that barn of a house. The house was supposed to be a big deal at one time—I don't know—some famous architect, but it was dated, you know? So I says to him, 'David,' that's his name David—'David, this house is too old. Tear it down.' But there was some sort of restriction on it by the Bluegrass Trust people, so we could only remodel. I don't mind, though, since we're not here except for the races and to check on David's horses, but there it is. Now it looks like I have to entertain, so I need cookware. I'm actually a good cook—if it's Italian, that is." Asa stuck her thumbnail in her mouth and looked thoughtful. "I guess I could hire a cook." She shrugged.

Deliah looked dazed by the stream of information spilling out of Asa's mouth. Her eyes had a glazed-over look, but what she did register was that the lady standing before her was RICH, which translated into a hefty sales commission! "One of our services is our referral list. If you like, I can give you contact information for very experienced chefs in the area who cater or will come to your house to cook for a dinner party. That way you're free to spend time with your guests."

"Perfect! I didn't want to schlep to the grocery store myself and cook for my husband's fat old friends anyway. Know what I mean?"

Deliah blinked and nodded, not knowing what else to do.

"I'll take that set over there," said Asa, pointing to a set of expensive cookware. "You've been such a doll. Gee, I've got that problem solved, but I've got another. My husband tells me this morning we've got to blend in more, so I need to find some worthy cause to throw some money at. My husband . . . David . . . that's his name, wants to make friends with the horsey people. You know of any worthy charity? Don't suggest anything to do with an illness. I can't abide being near sick people, you know? I want something with a little glamour for just a select few. Too bad Lexington doesn't have an amateur theater group. I have a knack for acting, you know. If I hadn't married David, I could have played the waitress in the new Jim Jarmusch film."

"Oh, but we do!" Deliah chimed in.

"No kidding."

"We have some fine acting groups in the Bluegrass. They put on wonderful plays."

"Sounds interesting."

"I know of a group that meets your standards if you are looking for Bluegrass aristocracy."

"Do tell."

Deliah looked downcast.

"What's the matter, honey?"

"I don't know if this group is still intact. We had an unfortunate situation not too long ago."

Asa pulled out her black American Express card. "Tell me about it. I hope it's juicy."

Not able to take her eyes off the exclusive Centurion card, Deliah lunged for it.

Asa brandished it out of Deliah's reach. "Story first. Then card."

Deliah leaned closer and in a conspiratorial tone whispered, "The lead in our next play died under suspicious circumstances."

"What do you mean?"

"Her name was Madison Smythe. You must have read about her in the paper. She died during a dress rehearsal. The funny thing is we were doing *The Murder*

Trap by Abigail Keam, in which the leading character dies of cyanide, and then our leading lady dies—they think of poison."

"That's terrible. Tell me more."

"The police arrested the props manager for the murder."

"Murder! Yikes. Why would I want to become a member of such a group?"

"I'm sorry. I thought you wanted to get cozy with the horsey set. Our group is made up of some of the oldest families in the Bluegrass. You can't get any bluer than these bluebloods."

"I see."

"I'm not supposed to gossip. It's rude."

"It *is* very rude, but this sounds like a group I'd like to join."

Deliah stalled. "I don't know."

Asa pulled out a hundred dollar bill from her wallet. "I'm very interested in this acting group. Sounds right up my alley."

"You gonna buy the cookware?"

"Yep, but I want some information to go along with the sale." Asa waved the hundred-dollar bill in front of Deliah's face.

As Deliah reached for it, Asa waved the bill out of reach. "Talk first." Asa knew waving money in front of Deliah was like teasing a cat with catnip, but she couldn't help herself. She had rarely seen such unbridled greed in someone so young, and it amused her.

Deliah looked around to see if the store manager was about. "Madison, that's the dead woman, was having an affair with one of the players—a Zion Foley."

"How do you know?"

"I caught them kissing in one of the upstairs bedrooms."

"Where?"

"At an estate called Wickliffe Manor. It was where we were staging the play."

"During one of the rehearsals?"

"Yes."

"Who else knew about them?"

"I know her husband did. I was making a discreet exit when John was coming up the stairs as I was going down. I must have had a strange expression on my face. John says to me, 'Where's the fire?' Then we both heard Madison laughing. John continued up, and I fled downstairs. I wanted to get out of pistol range."

"What happened?"

"I heard an argument and then a scuffle."

"What did the other actors do?"

"No one else was there yet. Just the four of us."

"Nobody else?"

"The owner Hunter Wickliffe was home."

"Where was this Hunter Wickliffe?"

"He was outside cutting down honeysuckle. He had

a chainsaw on, so he wouldn't have heard anything."

Asa looked impatiently at Deliah. "Well?"

"I heard Madison tell John she wanted a divorce. He yelled back that she could have it when she tore up the prenup. Otherwise, he was going to make trouble for her and Zion. John yelled at Zion to leave his wife alone." Deliah paused, glancing around the store.

"Don't stop now."

"There was a small scuffle. Something fell on the floor and then silence. I went into the kitchen to get a drink of water. When I came back into the parlor, Madison and Zion were practicing their lines, and John was coaching them as if nothing had happened."

"What did you do?"

"I acted like I hadn't heard anything, and asked John to help me with a scene. By this time, others were arriving."

"How long did this altercation occur before Madison's death?"

"About a month, I should think."

"Did you tell the other actors what you witnessed?"

"No. I wanted to stay clear of the entire shebang."

"Do you think the props manager had anything to do with Madison's death?"

"I don't know. He didn't like her, for sure, but it would seem her husband had more reason to kill Madison."

"Did you like Madison?"

Deliah's eyes brightened. "Sure. She was nice."

"Are you positive?" Asa leaned into her and said, "Don't lie to me, cutie pie. I can tell if you do."

Deliah bit her quivering bottom lip before answering. "I stayed away from her. She had a filthy temper."

Asa slipped the hundred-dollar bill down Deliah's cleavage. "Good girl. Now, let's buy some cookware."

25

"What's all this?" I asked.

"I thought your old pans looked kind of shabby, so I've replaced them," Asa replied.

My heart skipped a beat. "You didn't throw out my skillets, did ya?"

Asa muttered, "Throw out the sacred cast iron skillets? Not if I want to live."

"Asa, this is sweet, but I can't afford new cookware."

"They're a gift, Mother."

"I sure could use them. I know Eunice would love them. She keeps complaining that she has to bring her pots over, and she's tired of lugging them back and forth."

"I thought most of the cooking for the receptions was done in a certified kitchen."

"Shh. Don't ask. Don't tell."

Asa laughed. "I hope you don't get busted by the health department." Asa started washing the cookware.

"Of course, this kitchen is always spotless."

Baby padded into the kitchen, drool from the folds in his mouth slowly dripping onto the floor in long, disgusting strands. Ginger followed behind and began licking the floor.

"But then again," Asa lamented. "Ginger, stop that. Nasty."

I got a rag and wiped up the gooey mess and then fought with Baby to clean his face. He had bits of grass and leaves sticking out of his mouth. "Where in the world have you been?" I asked, prying his mouth open to make sure nothing sharp was in that cavern of his.

Baby pulled away and sneezed, leaving more of a gooey mess on the floor and me.

Asa cried, "Oh, gross."

"Can you clean this up while I change?" I asked, looking down at globs of snot on my shirt. "Baby, you make me so mad. Now I have to disinfect the counter and the floor."

Baby sneezed again for good measure and padded out to the great room to plop down in his bed on the slate floor. Ginger followed and lay on her bed next to Baby.

Asa got out the disinfectant and began wiping down surfaces. "You've got to do something with that dog, Mom."

"What would you have me do, Asa?"

"Can't you train him?"

"He's been to every obedience school in the Blue-grass. This is as good as it gets with Baby. Besides he's my friend, and he will always have a home with me. That brings up something. Asa, if anything should happen to me, make sure Baby is well taken care of. I want him to have a good home and be happy."

"What do you mean 'if anything should happen to you?'"

"You know."

"No, I don't know. Is there anything of which I should be aware?"

"Going outside one's front door is dangerous. I'm just saying—you know—in case I get sick or hit by a meteorite." I inspected my shoes, as I was unable to meet Asa's penetrating stare. I wasn't ready to tell her yet.

"Yes, Mother. I will make sure Baby and all your animals have happy homes."

"And the bees?"

"I will make sure the bees are well looked after. You needn't worry about them."

"We've never talked about the Butterfly."

"Mom, go change your shirt. I'm going to clean the kitchen. You're not going to die today or the next. We'll talk about this stuff later."

I didn't say it, but it had better be sooner than later.

26

Daniel Boone said he was never lost in the Kentucky wilderness during the 1700s, but was bewildered once for three days.

That's the way I felt sitting at a conference table in Shaneika's office looking at pictures on the walls. There were pictures of Shaneika with several US presidents. Pictures of Shaneika with Civil Rights activists. Pictures of Shaneika fly-fishing. Pictures of Shaneika with Comanche at various races. Pictures of Shaneika with famous horse trainers at Keeneland Race Track. Pictures of Shaneika receiving community awards. My girl Shaneika was coming up in the world.

But that's not what was bewildering me. It was piecing together what everyone said, and realizing none of it made any sense.

Shaneika went to the old school blackboard she had found at a garage sale, and picked up a piece of chalk. "Let's see what we've got, shall we? Asa, take the lead, please."

"When I interviewed Franklin, he stated that he was first to the house. Hunter was outside working in the yard. Franklin poured juice into the decanter and put both the cranberry bottle and decanter back in the fridge. The juice in the bottle did not look tampered with to him."

"Was it unsealed?" Shaneika inquired.

"Yes."

"So anyone could have gotten to it during those two days after Franklin first opened the cranberry juice bottle and that night?"

Asa replied, "Theoretically, yes. He put the empty goblets on the table in the parlor and went out back to talk with Hunter. When he came back, John was taking the decanter out of the fridge, and filled the goblets. But Franklin insists that *he* usually filled the goblets. He thought it odd John filled them that night."

Shaneika wrote quickly on the board and held up a hand to stop Asa. "Let me catch up, Asa." She wrote more facts down and stepped back, looking at the board. "Asa, who does Franklin place in the house now?"

"According to his statement, Madison was smoking on the terrace. Zion and Robin were in the dining room practicing their lines."

"Where was John Smythe?" Shaneika asked.

"After Smythe filled the goblets, Franklin's statement doesn't indicate where John went."

"Okay, what happened next?"

"Franklin took the decanter and goblets off the table, dusted it, and replaced the items."

I interjected, "I think this is very important."

"Why?" asked Shaneika.

Asa answered, "Robin told me John was very explicit about who was to pick up which goblet. Madison was always to pick up the one on the left, and Zion the right one."

Shaneika paused for a moment. "Why is that? What difference did it make which goblet they picked up?"

"Exactly," drawled Asa. "That's not all." She tossed two manuscripts on the table. "I bought Keam's play off the internet. There are no instructions about which character is to pick up which goblet."

Asa tapped on a second manuscript. "This is the manuscript John gave Mother."

I nodded in concurrence.

"It has instructions for who was to pick up which goblet and drink in the scene between Madison and Zion."

Shaneika grinned. "So someone inserted those instructions into the manuscript the cast was using."

"Madison might not have been the intended victim. It could have been Zion. When Franklin took the goblets and decanter off the table to dust, he might not have put the goblets back the same way John had arranged them."

"This gives me ammunition for probable doubt. I can punch holes in the DA's case." She looked at the board and wrote Motive—Grudge.

"Really?" I scoffed.

Shaneika replied, "People have killed for less, and I feel that's what the DA is going to go after."

"John has a stronger motive than Franklin," I said.

"We'll get to him in a moment," Shaneika replied, looking at the board. "Let's continue. What about Robin Russell?"

Asa leaned forward and placed her elbows on the table. "I wouldn't count on anything Robin has to say. She is giving conflicting statements. Mother thinks she might have a medical condition, and even called her husband to suggest he make a doctor's appointment for her."

"Tell me anyway."

"The most important thing she said was that she put a blanket on Madison after Hunter laid her on the couch and smelled burnt almonds," recounted Asa, reaching for a bottle of water placed on the table.

"That would indicate cyanide poisoning, but it's not how Madison died. I got the ME's report this morning. Madison died of cardiac arrest due to ingestion of ethylene glycol. She had calcium oxalate crystals in her kidneys, which indicated she was poisoned over an extended period, and then she was given a massive dose that night."

"Someone should notify Zion to see if he has these crystals, since both he and Madison were drinking the cranberry juice," Asa cautioned.

Shaneika warned, "Anyone who drank unsealed liquids from Hunter's fridge should be tested for ethylene glycol poisoning. That means you too, Josiah."

I looked in shock at Asa. "So it wasn't cyanide. It was antifreeze. The cranberry juice was a perfect cover because antifreeze tastes sweet. This might explain Madison's erratic behavior during the rehearsals."

Asa nodded. "Have the police checked Madison's home for antifreeze?"

"Yes, and they found nothing. Their theory was that Madison was being poisoned at Wickliffe Manor only. That's why they arrested Franklin."

"Which means Robin Russell is full of beans," concurred Asa. "Whatever she smelled, it wasn't burnt almonds."

I asked, "Whose fingerprints were on the cranberry juice bottle?"

Shaneika thumbed through several police reports and picked up one. "The police could not lift any identifiable prints. They were too smudged. They do believe, however, based on witness statements, that John handled the juice bottle. Franklin also admitted he poured the juice into the decanter."

I doodled on a notepad, feeling quite depressed. I had thought Madison a witch, but she was probably acting out due to the effects of the ethylene glycol. During all those rehearsals, Madison was gradually being murdered in front of our eyes, and no one recognized it.

Shaneika said encouragingly, "Let's look at Robin's statement."

"She's a waste of time," I asserted.

"The DA might not think so. He might be very selective about Robin's memories from that night he uses. Let's go over it."

"Okay," Asa said.

I nodded.

"Asa, you start."

"I talked to her first. She claimed Franklin confided to her that Madison was pinching things from the house. She also claims she saw John Smythe stealing a jade trinket from the hallway and stuffing it into a pocket of Madison's coat, which was hanging in the hallway."

"Did Franklin ever confide to Robin about the thefts?"

"He told me," I answered.

Asa replied, "He said he mentioned it to Hunter as well."

"But not to Robin?"

Asa shook her head and said, "She claims he did."

Shaneika looked at me. "What about you?"

"When I talked to her, Robin confirmed that John

did place the decanter and goblets on the table. Then she claimed she smelled burnt almonds on Madison's breath."

Shaneika shuffled through a report. "According to my notes, she said she put a blanket on Madison. She also claimed Zion put a blanket on her. Don't you mean 'over' her, as in covering a deceased person?"

"That's a problem right there. I don't remember Madison being covered with a blanket. There wasn't a blanket in the play, and we were downstairs. Where would the blanket have come from?"

"Josiah, are you saying there was no blanket?" Shaneika asked.

"I'm saying I don't remember a blanket."

"But you stated Hunter picked Madison off the floor and put her back on the couch," Asa declared.

"Yeah, that's right. We thought Madison had a stroke or something. I wasn't thinking murder at the time, and neither was Hunter, I'm sure."

"So, someone could have put a blanket over Madison later, out of respect," Asa mused while studying me.

"I just don't remember a blanket."

Shaneika wrote on the board for Robin—NO MOTIVE. "Let's move on. What about this college kid Ashley Moore?"

Asa was the first to speak up. "I checked. Robin did have a baby at the tender age of fifteen. Now, whether this boy is her son, I don't know. It sounds to me like he is trying to shake her down for money."

"So, we don't have the real story about him. Asa, can you gather some DNA evidence on this guy and compare it to Robin?" asked Shaneika.

"I'll get one of my guys on it. Don't worry. Ashley and Robin will never realize a DNA sample has been collected. My people are good."

"Good. Let's leave Ashley blank since we don't know enough about him. Josiah, you said you left the room to get Madison water and a towel."

"Yes, I went into the kitchen."

"That's when you heard a commotion."

"Correct."

"Who was in the room?"

"Let me think for a moment. Franklin passed me in the hallway, rushing to find Hunter. When I got to the parlor, everyone was there. Zion, Robin, Deliah, Ashley, and John."

"Anyone else?"

"A few more players straggled in after the fact."

Shaneika shoved a lawyer's notepad at me. "Write down their names and contact info, please."

I did what she instructed and handed back the pad.

Shaneika looked appraisingly at the board. "This is looking good for Franklin. There's enough inconsistency here to drive a truck through. Let's get to Deliah Webster. Asa, I think you talked to her."

"Yes, I did. Where to start with that one? I don't know how well this Deliah would play on the witness stand."

Shaneika pursed her lips. "She's not credible?"

"She's a flaky sexpot on the make. I think women on the jury would resent her."

"She's a nice girl," I countered.

Asa continued, "She did confirm Zion and Madison were having an affair, and that John caught them."

"How did she know they were doing the nasty?" Shaneika asked.

"She discovered them kissing upstairs. John found them a few minutes later. Deliah claims she heard Madison ask John for a divorce, and he said he would give her one when she tore up his prenup. He then told Zion to leave his wife alone."

Shaneika smiled. "Oh, this is gold. Pure gold." She wrote under John's name—MOTIVE-Money/Jealousy "I will dress little Miss Sexpot in a nun's outfit if I have to, but this gal will testify. If this doesn't create doubt in a juror's mind, I don't know what will."

I added, "I can testify Zion admitted to me that he was having an affair with Madison. I think he genuinely cared for her."

Shaneika wrote under Zion's name—MOTIVE-Jealousy/Revenge. "Perhaps he was frustrated because Madison wouldn't divorce John, or maybe she told him to get lost." Shaneika looked at the board, almost purring.

Asa advanced another possibility. "Let's not forget Madison might not have been the target. It is feasible John put the antifreeze in the cranberry juice to kill Zion, his rival."

I mused, "If John put antifreeze in the juice bottle, then he intended to kill both Madison and Zion."

"There's a problem with that angle," Asa said. "If John was really after Madison's money, why murder her in front of witnesses? He would have known there would be a full-blown investigation."

"What about insurance money?" asked Shaneika.

Asa shrugged. "Still working on it."

"If there are insurance policies on Madison or Zion, I want to know about it, and who's paying the premiums."

Asa saluted. "Yes, ma'am!"

I stood up. "Ladies, I'm going home. I'm tired. This whole thing is distressing."

Asa and Shaneika exchanged glances.

Shaneika offered, "Sure, Josiah, go home. I can have one of my people drive you."

Asa gathered her notes and placed them in a briefcase. "No, I'll drive Mother home. You do look a little tired, Mom."

"I feel a nap coming on."

Asa picked up my purse and handed my silver-headed wolf's cane to me.

I was exhausted. And it wasn't even lunchtime yet.

27

There was a knock on the door.

I was sleeping on the couch, and unsteadily got up to answer it, almost tripping over Baby, who was napping beside me on the floor. I looked at my monitor and pulled back in surprise. I opened the door and said, "Hello, Hunter."

"May I come in?"

I hesitated for a moment. "Hunter, I've got to be honest. If it is about us, I'm not up to hearing it. I am plumb worn out."

"It is about us, but not the way you're thinking."

"Do us both a favor. Write me a Dear Jane letter and leave it at that."

"What are you going on about? I'm here to explain why I haven't been around lately."

"It doesn't matter. We didn't have much of a chance anyway."

"Oh, shut up," Hunter groused as he pushed past me.

Baby and Ginger rose, padding over to Hunter to be petted.

"Hey, Baby's clean for a change."

"I bathed him last night. Don't worry. He'll get dirty again as soon as I let him out."

Hunter went into the kitchen and opened the fridge. He poured two glasses of iced tea and brought them into the great room. "Sit down."

I sat on the couch and moved my afghan out of his way.

Sipping on his iced tea, Hunter glanced around. "This is some house. Good bones."

"Quit stalling. What's this all about?"

"I want to apologize for not being more attentive."

"You've had a lot on your plate."

"Before that. I stopped coming around. Didn't call."

"You don't need to explain, Hunter."

"Yes, I do." He took another sip. "I guess I better tell you. I'm broke, Josiah. I don't mean broke as in homeless, but if things keep going the way they are, that might be in the cards." He chuckled, but it was not a haha chuckle. It was more like a "oh, my gosh" chuckle—"can this be happening to me?"

I didn't say anything, but I saw fear in Hunter's eyes the same way I saw fear in the mirror when I looked at myself several years ago.

"I am mired in debt, and I'm going to have to sell Wickliffe Manor to get out of it."

"I'm very sorry to hear that, Hunter. Truly I am." I reached for his hand.

"I didn't have the money to take you out, so I didn't call. I was embarrassed, and frazzled from trying to restore the place."

"You should have told me. We don't need money to have a good time. We could have watched a movie on TV, swum in my pool, or confiscated Lady Elsmere's pontoon boat and floated down the Kentucky River bird watching. We could have stuck her with the gas bill."

Hunter smiled. "A man should take his lady out. A man who can't take his date out on the town is a bum."

"This situation does not define who you are, Hunter. It's just your current circumstance. You'll pull yourself out of this."

"I've made arrangements to sell the Hanoverian."

"No, you're not! Absolutely no way. I will not allow it. I'll cover the horse's expenses until you get back on your feet. The horse stays here. Besides, what would Morning Glory do without her buddy?"

"I'm afraid I won't be much fun until this situation with Franklin is resolved."

"How is he doing? I haven't talked to him since that horrible fight with Matt."

"Not good, Josiah. Franklin is staying with me for now. He goes to work. His boss likes Franklin and hasn't fired him, but Franklin mopes about Matt."

"He'd better concentrate on his predicament and forget about Matt."

"What is it with Matt?"

I sighed. "I don't know. Franklin is so good for him, but Matt doesn't see it. I can tell you that I love Matt, but I'm ashamed of his behavior toward Franklin."

"I'd like to bust Matt in the chops."

"Someone say my name?"

Hunter and I looked up from our conversation to see Matt walk into the room holding Emmeline.

Matt seemed startled to see Hunter. "Excuse me, Josiah. I didn't realize you have company."

Hunter rose.

"Don't," I warned. "The baby."

"Is there something you want to say to me, Hunter?" Matt asked.

"I didn't come here for you. I came to see Jo."

"Like I said—excuse me." Matt started for his room.

"You're not even going to ask about Franklin?" Hunter asked, astounded.

"Not with the baby around. I can tell you're itching for a fight, Hunter, but it will have to be another time. I won't give you any satisfaction when my daughter is present."

"Give her to Josiah, and let's continue this conversation outside."

Matt ignored Hunter and, stepping into his bedroom, closed and locked the door.

"Can you believe that guy!" Hunter exclaimed.

"He's doing you a favor."

"What do you mean?"

"Matt is some twenty years younger, plus he has about thirty pounds on you, and believe me, it's all muscle."

"I can handle myself."

"I'm sure you can, but Matt can also. Hunter, simmer down. This macho stuff is not going to bring Franklin and Matt back together."

"I can't stand that guy. I've got to go. I don't want to be in the same house with him."

"Okay," I replied, but I was saying it to thin air.

Hunter had already left and slammed the front door.

I gave out a big sigh. *That sure went well,* I mused to myself. I could see that if the rift between Franklin and Matt was not repaired, I might lose both of them, because Hunter would make me choose.

That was one decision I didn't want to make.

Not at all!

28

Kentucky has had its share of spectacular murders—ones that stick in your craw and don't let go. We even had our share of serial killers before people knew there was such a thing.

In 1824, one Isaac Desha was staying at a tavern near Mays Lick, Kentucky. He met a man from Mississippi named Francis Baker and accompanied the traveler on his way to visit Mr. Baker's friend in the area. Both men left the tavern on their respective horses, but Francis Baker never arrived at his friend's house.

Instead, Mr. Baker was later found in the woods under some brush with bludgeon wounds to his head, stab wounds in his chest and shoulders, and his throat cut. Evidently, Mr. Baker was hard to kill.

Desha was arrested after his personal effects were found near Baker's body, and Desha had possession of Baker's horse, which he had previously admired.

It didn't help Desha that after Baker's murder and

before his arrest, Desha's pregnant wife left him, never to return. What had she seen or heard causing her to run?

Not to worry, though. Desha's father was Joseph Desha, the ninth governor of Kentucky, and he pardoned his son after two trials where Isaac was pronounced guilty. It seems Governor Desha couldn't get the verdict he wanted, so he took it upon himself to save his son.

If there was any doubt about Isaac's predilection for murder, it was wiped away when he fled to Texas, where he murdered another traveling pilgrim. He died before that trial started, and his death made national news. One newspaper wrote, "The world, it appears, is at last relieved from the presence of the notorious . . . Desha."

I've always believed there is something in the rich Kentucky soil that can bring out the worst in us. After all, Kentucky has always been called "the dark and bloody ground," because the land is soaked with the blood of innocent and sinner alike. Cherokees, Shawnees, Mingos, Yuchis, Chickasaws, Wyandots, Delawares, Miamis, French fur traders, explorers, tradesmen, British soldiers, American frontiersmen, African-American slaves, horse thieves, Confederate soldiers, Union soldiers, striking coal miners, clan feuds, and the tobacco wars have seen their fair share of brutal violence.

I don't know why I was thinking of Isaac Desha at Madison's funeral. I was sitting on a hard wooden pew inside a small, limestone church, listening to a minister drone on about how wonderful Madison was.

We all knew she wasn't, but I guess that was beside the point. I was comparing Madison's murder to that of Francis Baker's. What drove Isaac Desha to murder a stranger he met at a tavern? To steal the man's horse?

He must have known he would be caught and eventually tried for murder.

Why did Isaac Desha kill? Was it a compulsion? Personal gain? To rob Francis Baker of his horse and money, Desha had to rob the man of his life. And it was such a sloppy murder. Blood was found on both horses and Desha's clothes. Desha was in possession of Baker's horse, and Desha's personal effects were discovered around Baker's hidden corpse. Then there is the matter of Desha's pregnant wife fleeing her home. Women did not leave their husbands in 1824 unless it was a matter of extreme necessity. What did Isaac say to her or was it the blood on his clothes that made her panic and run?

Personal gain. Personal gain. Personal gain.

Isaac Desha killed for personal gain. Of course, it was more than that for him. Isaac Desha was a predator. Look at the viciousness of the murder. He only used robbery as an excuse to kill, and he would have gone on killing until he was stopped in Texas.

But was personal gain the motive for Madison's murder?

I rubbernecked at those attending. John was in the front pew bawling his eyes out. He was so good at exhibiting grief, I almost believed he loved Madison.

The murderer had to be John Smythe. He was the only one who really benefited from her death—all that luscious money.

To my left sat Ashley Moore with Deliah Webster. Hmm, what was going on there? Anything? Nothing?

Up near the front sat Peter Russell, but Robin was absent. I hoped she was feeling all right.

Zion was in the very back, drunk, and mumbling incoherently.

I discreetly got up, went to the rear of the church, and called for a taxi. Then I sat beside Zion. "Come on, Zion. This is not the time for acting like a fool."

"Leave me alone," Zion sneered, pulling away from me.

I tugged on his arm and whispered, "Think about what you're doing."

He started weeping. "He cremated her, Jo. He burned her up. All that loveliness gone. It makes me sick to think of it."

"I know, Zion."

"I didn't even get to see Madison one last time."

"Let's go outside and talk. Come on, Zion. Let the others mourn in their own way."

I gently tugged at his arm again, and this time, he followed.

We sat on a bench under a massive oak tree.

Zion kicked at broken acorns lying on the ground. "Looks like the squirrels got these," he murmured. Zion looked at the gloomy sky, wiped his tear-stained face, and asked, "Is it going to be okay, Jo?"

I put my arm around his shoulder and pulled him close. "I don't know, Zion, but I can tell you this. Grief doesn't go away, but it's possible to reach the point where you can live with it."

"Do you miss Brannon?"

"Sometimes. There have been nights when I think I hear him rummaging in the kitchen, and I call out his name."

"I know things got messy at the end."

"Yes, they did," I replied, thinking of Brannon stealing from me, cheating on me, and then abandoning me. He threw me on the garbage pile without so much as a kiss-my-fanny.

"Madison and I had a future together. A real future."

I didn't respond, since I believed they would have been divorced within two years if they had married. It was one of those rare times I showed restraint. Nice of me, don't you think?

"It's better to have loved and lost than never to have loved at all."

"Ah, Jo, that's such crap."

"You're right. I was trying to help you feel better, Zion. You're going through a terrible hurt right now, and there's nothing anybody can do to help you. You just have to struggle through it."

Zion started crying again, so I handed him my handkerchief. He blew his nose and crammed my good linen hanky in his pocket.

Oh, well.

"Jo, did you notice Robin wasn't here?"

"Yes. I hope she's okay. Robin was acting a little goofy the last time I saw her. Not herself at all."

"You know she's a drinker."

"No, I didn't realize. How do you know?"

"That jumbo thermos she brings to all the rehearsals. You think it's filled with tea. Hell, no. It's full of sangria."

"You must be mistaken, Zion. She chugs from that thermos like a baby sucking milk from its mother."

"Exactly. I'm telling you, Robin is on her way to becoming a full-blown alcoholic. Madison and I sneaked drinks with her during rehearsals. I'm telling you that gigantic thermos was full of sangria."

"Zion, your cab is here." I helped Zion up and over to the cab. After getting him stowed away in the back seat, I gave the driver Zion's address and bid them both goodbye. I stood watching the cab pull out onto the highway before I made my way back into the church.

Somehow the mention of that thermos filled with sangria stayed on my mind. I couldn't shake it.

What did it mean?

29

The service was over. I sat in a pew in the back of the church, waiting for everyone else to leave. I'm slow, and I don't like to hold people up with my bad leg . . . and neither do they.

Peter Russell stopped by my pew. "Hi Josiah. Nasty business, eh?"

"It is an unhappy day, for sure. How's Robin?"

"Not doing too good. She didn't feel up to coming."

"Did she go to the doctor?"

Peter buttoned his coat. "Yeah, but we're still waiting on the test results."

"Give her my regards, will you?"

"Sure. Well, I've got to go. Robin might need me."

"Bye."

I was about to follow Peter out when John Smythe headed straight for me after speaking with several well-wishers. Widowed and divorced women were offering condolences and a shoulder to cry on if needed.

Madison had barely been put to rest, and already the buzzards were encircling John, making a bid to be the next Mrs. Smythe. He shooed them away deftly before sidling alongside me.

"Josiah, I saw how you got Zion out of here before he made a scene. I want to thank you."

I nodded. I didn't know what to say, and I didn't want to be sitting alone with John inside an empty church.

"I appreciate you coming, considering your feelings for Franklin."

"I believe he's innocent."

"I realize that." He scooted closer.

I scanned the church to see if anyone else was still inside. Fortunately, there were several parishioners lighting candles and praying.

"Little birdies have told me that Asa is investigating the case for Franklin's lawyer."

"She's been poking around," I confirmed.

"I've never had the pleasure of meeting your daughter. She hasn't interviewed me."

"She'll get around to it."

"What does she look like, so I'll know it's her?"

"She looks like a bird of prey."

John laughed, then stopped short after looking at the sour expression on my face. "Tell her I had nothing to do with the death of my late wife. I loved her."

"There are witnesses who say Madison wanted a divorce."

"Madison had been under a strain while doing *The Murder Trap*. She wasn't herself."

"Did you take the cranberry juice out of the fridge and fill the decanter?"

"No, Franklin did, but I filled the goblets. I've already talked to Detective Kelly about this. I have nothing to hide. I know Franklin's your friend, but he must have slipped the antifreeze into the juice while he was dusting the table."

"Why did you hide a jade knickknack in Madison's coat pocket?"

John bristled at the question. His soft, pudgy body quivered in righteous indignation. He pushed his limp, dirty blond hair away from his eyes. "I did no such thing. Whoever accused me of such atrocious behavior is lying!"

He stood quickly. "I just wanted to thank you for helping with Zion. Tell Asa I'm innocent. She doesn't need to question me."

"I'll tell her, but I don't think it will do much good. Asa's relentless. She'll track you down sooner or later."

I watched him hurry out of the church and gave him a few moments to get to his car and drive away. What a phony baloney John was. He was trying to get information out of me, but I turned the tables on him. *Wanted to thank me for helping with Zion.* What crap! John hated Zion, and must have been delighted when Zion showed up drunk to the funeral, so the attendees would sympathize with the grieving widower.

I hope he had sleepless nights now, like Franklin was having. He was going to obsess over who had seen him steal the jade statuette.

Yes, I was mad at John because of Franklin, but after seeing him grieve at Madison's funeral, I wasn't so sure he'd killed her. He seemed broken up about the death of his wife. I didn't think his grief was fake.

After all, he was a director. Not an actor. He was worse at acting than I was. And that's saying something.

30

"I don't care who the real murderer is. My job is to put enough reasonable doubt in the jury's mind to acquit."

"But why does Franklin have to go to trial if he doesn't need to?"

"That's not my job, Josiah."

"Isn't your job to protect your client?" I turned to my daughter. "Asa, help me here."

"You're doing fine, Mom."

Shaneika shot Asa a nasty look. "You're not believing this crazy theory of your mother's, are you?"

"Now listen to me, Shaneika. Madison had a massive dose of ethylene glycol that night. How did it get into her system? She had to ingest it somehow."

"Right. From the cranberry juice."

"No." I slapped the table. Jumping Jehosaphat! I hurt my broken finger. I rummaged through the reports on her desk. "Here. Here. This one." I opened the file folder and spilled out photos, pointing at one.

"Now look. What do you see?"

"The table with decanter and the goblets."

"What else do you see? Look closer. Asa, do you see it?"

"Yes, Mother. I know."

"Someone clue me in, because I see the decanter and two goblets, one of which Madison drank from and . . . oh, my goodness!" Shaneika leaned in for a closer look. "Why didn't I notice this before?"

"Because we were set up to 'see' a certain way." I turned to Asa. "You know who did this, don't you?"

"Yes, but I can't prove it yet."

"Will you be able to?"

"Yes, I think I can. I've suspected for some time. It was a clever attempt. The murderer almost got away with it."

"Will you tell me what you're talking about?" Shaneika pleaded.

"In due time," Asa replied with a smug smile. "In due time."

31

Franklin had lost a lot of weight, and his face looked haggard. He had a faint stubble on his cheeks, and his clothes were disheveled.

"You look like crap, Frankie boy," I said when he opened the door of Wickliffe Manor.

"It's nice to see you, too." He looked at the casserole pan in my hands. "That for me?"

"You and your brother. Hunter around?"

"He's out back working."

"Go get him and wash up. I've got lasagna, salad, and garlic bread."

"Who died?"

"You will if you don't eat a decent meal. Now, scoot. I'll bring everything in."

"Is the lasagna homemade?"

"I also made a Devil's Food chocolate cake with marshmallow icing, which I'm going to take back if you give me any more lip."

"I'm off to see the Wizard." Franklin hurried down

the hallway and out to the backyard.

I brought the food into the kitchen, including the cake. Rummaging through the drawers, I found the good sterling silverware and linen napkins. The lasagna was cool, so I placed it in the oven along with the garlic bread to toast.

Hurrying into the formal dining room, I set the table with Hunter's finest china and crystal glasses. Suddenly, I heard footsteps running up the back stairs. I smiled, because I knew it was Hunter and Franklin rushing to clean up for dinner. Seeing as I had a few moments to spare, I went outside and cut a wildflower bouquet to place on the table.

I was setting the vase on the mahogany dining table when Hunter rushed into the room, tucking his shirttail into his pants. His hair was wet. I noticed Hunter was letting it grow out a bit. It looked sexy.

"What's the occasion, Josiah?"

"I know the two of you are keeping close to home nowadays, and if I wanted to see you, I had to come here. Also, I know you must be starving."

Franklin called from the kitchen. "Josiah, the garlic bread is getting brown."

"Take it out then," I yelled. "Bring in the salad from the fridge, will ya?"

Hunter went to help Franklin bring the food into the dining room. It wasn't long before we were sitting at the table and stuffing our mouths full of red wine, warm garlic bread, homemade lasagna, and crisp salad.

"This is too much," Franklin jabbered with his mouth full. He swallowed and made a big gulping sound. "It's been a long time since Hunter and I had a nice meal."

Hunter took a sip of wine. "I don't cook unless I can grill it." He looked fondly at Franklin. "My baby brother can cook when he's in the mood."

"I've been too upset to cook lately, but I can make a mean shrimp and grits." Franklin wiped his mouth. "This hits the spot."

"I'm glad I could help," I declared.

Hunter asked, "Speaking of helping, has Asa found anything?"

Franklin looked at me expectantly.

"Shaneika thinks she can put a bulldozer through holes in the DA's case."

Franklin put down his fork. "That's not enough, Josiah. I've got to be proven innocent. I can't go through life with people thinking I killed a woman."

"Asa's doing all she can to prove your innocence."

"I'm sorry if I come across as pushy and ungrateful. I'm not, you know."

"Franklin, we're doing everything possible."

Hunter admonished, "Franklin, move on."

"Okay. How's Emmeline?"

"Growing like a weed."

Franklin looked as though he was on the verge of

tears, but refrained at the last moment. "And?"

"Matt is miserable. Just plumb miserable."

Franklin's face brightened.

Hunter threw his napkin on the table. "How can you inquire about that jerk?"

Franklin shrugged. "It was good between Matt and me in the beginning, wasn't it, Josiah?"

I nodded. "I first met you when you came to the hospital with Matt to see me."

"Why were you in the hospital?" Hunter asked.

"It's so long ago, I can't recall, but I dimly remember a priest came to my room and gave me the last rites."

Franklin and I both tittered while Hunter seemed confused.

"That was a terrible time for me, but I got through it, Franklin, and you will get through this. I promise."

"I concur. You will, Franklin," Hunter added encouragingly. He glanced at his empty plate. "Enough of this maudlin talk. I'm stuffed, but just happen to have enough room left for a piece of cake."

Franklin pushed back his chair. "I'll get the dessert plates and Mother's fancy dessert forks." He removed our dirty plates and carried them into the kitchen.

"I've got some vanilla ice cream in the freezer," Hunter suggested.

"I'll get it," I offered. "You sit and digest your meal."

"Are you trying to spoil me, Miss Josiah? It's working."

"I know what it's like to be under tremendous stress. A nice meal with friends can turn a horrible day into a tolerable one."

"I spend my work days around crime sites and the worst of humanity. Sometimes I forget people can be decent."

"Have you told Franklin you're going to sell Wickliffe Manor?"

"Not yet. I'll wait until after the trial. I can hang on until then. There is no point burdening him with this, too. Please don't tell him."

"I won't."

Franklin burst into the dining carrying three delicate porcelain plates and forks. "Found them. They were dusty, so I had to wash them."

That gave me an idea. "Franklin, when you dusted the table before Madison's episode, did you wipe down the decanter and the goblets as well?"

"Probably. I like crystal to reflect the light."

"That explains it."

Hunter asked, "Explains what?"

"Why John Smythe's fingerprints weren't on the glassware."

Hunter snapped his fingers. "Of course. Why didn't I think of that?"

"Because you're too emotionally involved to look at

this case with unbiased eyes."

"You mean I wiped both our prints off when I cleaned the glassware, and then put my prints back on when I placed them back on the end table?"

"Exactly. You cleaned the glassware when you dusted the table and then handled the goblets and decanter again to put them back on the table. That's why there was only one set of prints."

"I feel sick."

"Franklin, you had no way of knowing you were destroying evidence. A crime had not been committed yet. Don't worry. Shaneika will make mincemeat of the DA's theory."

"Yes, Franklin, don't worry. I've had to testify in cases where Shaneika cross-examined me. She's tough. I mean really tough."

"I wonder," Franklin said.

I wondered too, but cut the cake while Hunter scooped out ice cream. We were quiet eating our dessert, because the three of us could feel Damocles' sword hanging over Franklin's head. Would it fall and cut his throat?

That was the question, but what was the answer?

32

"Robin, what happened?" I asked, moving a chair closer to her hospital bed. It was one of those newfangled hospital rooms where there was an additional area in the room for a family member to sleep. Besides a regular bathroom with a walk-in shower large enough for a wheelchair, there was a sink area in the room as well. I guess it was for the medical personnel to wash their hands before leaving the room.

"Josiah, it's good of you to come."

"What happened?" I asked again.

"They tell me I collapsed in church. When I woke up, I was here."

"Do they know what's wrong?"

"The doctors keep scratching their heads. I hope they figure it out soon. I want to go home."

"I brought you flowers from the Butterfly."

"That's very sweet. Can you put them on the dresser?"

"Sure." I rose and put the vase of flowers where

Robin could easily see them. "Flowers always brighten a hospital room."

"Yes, they do."

I sat back in the chair. "Is there anything I can do for you?"

"My memory is very fuzzy, but did something happen to Madison Smythe?"

"You don't remember?"

Robin shook her head.

"She died, Robin. You were there when it happened."

"I was?"

"Yes, dear."

"When is she going to be buried?"

"She's been put to rest."

Robin's face turned a bright red. She cried out, "What's happening to me that I can't remember something like that!" She burst into tears.

"Robin, I'm so sorry," I said, handing her a box of tissues.

"My mind has been in such a fog. I can't remember much of the past several months. I think I must be losing my mind."

"Have you had a MRI?"

"It was normal, but how do you explain this lack of memory?"

"Robin, do you remember getting a telephone call from the police asking you to get tested for calcium oxalate crystals?"

"Heavens, Josiah. Are you pestering my bride?"

In walked Peter Russell, Robin's husband, a tall, strapping giant of a man carrying a milkshake. He was an assistant professor at a local college and taught biology. "Here, baby, I got this for you."

Robin smiled weakly and reached for the milkshake, saying, "You're too good to me."

"Chocolate and thick, just the way you like it," he said before casting his baby blues at me. "Can I get you anything, Josiah? It's so nice of you to visit."

"I was just asking Robin if she has been tested for calcium oxalate crystals."

"Have I, honey?" Robin asked before taking a sip of her milkshake.

"I don't know." Peter directed his gaze at me. "Is there a reason why she should?"

"The police want everyone in the theater group to be tested."

"The police?" Peter asked, wearing a sudden frown. "Does this have anything to do with Madison?"

"Yes," I replied, but before I could say anything else, Peter squelched my line of inquiry. "I think this entire episode about Madison is what has made Robin ill. She was fine until that night at Wickliffe Manor."

"What are calcium oxalate crystals?" asked Robin, putting the milkshake on the nightstand next to her.

I waited for Peter to answer.

"I'll have a talk with the doctors about testing you

for them," he promised.

"Can these crystals be making me sick?" Robin asked.

"Let's change the subject. The doctors say Robin needs rest, and this talk of Madison raises her stress level." Peter glanced angrily at me.

"You know I was feeling queasy weeks before then, Peter."

"Before when, babe? You never said you weren't feeling well."

"I'm embarrassed to say this, but at first I thought it was due to Wickliffe Manor. I seemed to always feel bad after our rehearsals. I thought the house might have black mold or something I was allergic to, but nobody else seemed to suffer. Then I thought it was side effects due to my drinking. Josiah, please don't breathe a word of this, but Peter and I were having financial difficulties, so I was drinking at the time. I was heavily imbibing sangrias. Drinking was a release for me."

"I understand, Robin. I've had a few nips in my time." You will notice that I didn't promise I would keep quiet about this new piece of information.

Peter said, "Robin, I think we should tell your doctor about this."

"You do it, hon. I'm suddenly tired."

"Don't you want your milkshake? You say the ice cream settles your stomach."

"Not now. I want to sleep." Robin closed her eyes and drifted off.

I stood. "Is this normal?"

Peter checked his phone messages before speaking. "I don't know what to do, Josiah. I feel helpless. Robin keeps getting worse, and the doctors can't tell us what is wrong." After putting his phone away, Peter picked up the milkshake and flushed the contents down the toilet before straightening up the rest of Robin's private hospital room. I took this as my cue to leave.

"Peter, you have my number. Call if I can do anything for you."

Peter grunted goodbye while rinsing the milkshake container out in the sink.

I was genuinely sorry to see Robin so ill, but it was time for me to leave.

So I did.

33

My electronic gate was open. The mere sight of it not closed alarmed and irritated me as I drove down my gravel driveway. What fresh hell was this? You know me. I am paranoid to the max. Well, haven't I had reason to be?

I continued down my driveway cautiously, and then saw the reason for the gate being unlocked. An enormous, gaudy white limousine was parked in the middle of the road in front of Matt's cottage.

Matt was leaning on the vehicle watching Meriah play with Emmeline on the front lawn.

Well, wonders never cease.

Another man wearing a navy suit stood with Matt observing Meriah.

Matt strolled over to my car as I rolled down my window.

"What's going on?" I asked.

"This is Meriah's court-appointed visitation with Emmeline."

"So she is really taking you to court?"

"Looks like it."

"Who's the suit?"

"Her lawyer."

"I don't recognize him. From here?"

"Los Angeles."

"This is costing a pretty penny."

"I had my lawyer petition the court to have Meriah psychologically evaluated before she could see Emmeline again."

I peered around Matt at Meriah. I was still miffed about my tussle with her and my broken finger. I didn't want Meriah on the property, but I wasn't going to make waves at the moment. I could tell Matt was very tense.

"What did the evaluation say?"

"Never happened. That slick piece of work over there had the petition thrown out."

"Oh, dear."

"Oh, dear, indeed. The only consolation I got was that the visits must be in Lexington and supervised. Your police report on Meriah is the reason the judge agreed to that. Without it, Meriah would have had carte blanche to do as she pleases."

"This must be costing Meriah a fortune."

"She's rich, remember. Josiah, I don't have the money to fight her. I've got to find a way to solve this custody issue without spending myself into the poorhouse, but if that is what it takes, I'll gladly do it."

"You should have another witness while Meriah is here. She and her lawyer could say anything they wanted to the court about this visit. I'm sure that's why he's here. Let me pull over. I'll just sit in my car, but at least you'll have someone on your side if something goes haywire."

Matt looked relieved. "You can sit on the porch where it's cooler."

"No, thank you. It might disturb Meriah."

Matt glanced back at Meriah playing with Emmeline on a blanket in the yard. "I know you never cared much for Meriah, but she is, in truth, an amazing person. I wouldn't be here if it wasn't for her help after I was shot. I regret that we are at cross-purposes over Emmeline. Bitterly regret it."

"I warned you she might change her mind about Emmeline."

"I remember."

"If Meriah is such a wonderful person, why didn't you marry her when you were in California recuperating?"

"I thought about it, but I realized I was bound to walk away at some point. I hated Los Angeles and missed the Bluegrass." Matt paused for a moment. "I also missed Franklin."

"Then you need to do something about him."

"I intend to, as soon as this custody issue is over."

"I hope it won't be too late, Matt. Some people get one chance at love. You are way over your limit." I didn't want to talk to Matt anymore, so I rolled up my window and pulled my car over to keep an eye out until Meriah left.

Matt went back to lean on the limousine.

I could tell he was thinking about what I had said. I do hope he took it to heart and didn't throw away his chance at happiness. Whether it be Meriah or Franklin, Matt had to make a decision—and soon.

34

Asa handed each man a sealed envelope. "Make sure you hand-deliver these invitations to the person whose name is on the envelope and wait. It is of vital importance that they show up at the time listed on the invitation."

"What if they resist?" asked one of the men wearing aviator sunglasses, a black suit, and black tie.

"You know what to do. Make sure they arrive on time."

"Yes, ma'am," they replied in unison.

35

I was sitting next to Deliah in the very room where Madison Smythe died. The room had been taped off, but the yellow tape now lay on the floor in a careless mess. Nine chairs were arranged in a circle. So far, Deliah and I were the only ones present.

Deliah leaned over and whispered, "What's this all about?"

"I don't know."

Deliah sniffed the air and turned her nose up as though smelling something unpleasant like cow manure on the bottom of her pointy shoes.

We sat quietly reflecting until we heard a car pull up. Swiveling, we looked toward the front door, which had been left open. In stomped Zion, looking drained. He paused in the hallway, glanced about, and, upon seeing us, trudged over. "I was told that if I didn't show up, I'd be arrested."

"Some guy appeared at my work and handed me a note saying I had to come. He unnerved me, to say the least," Deliah commiserated.

"Josiah?" Zion inquired.

"I haven't a clue." I pulled an invitation out of my purse. "I got the same summons as you two did."

"Who's behind this?" Zion asked.

"I don't know." I did know who was behind this, but I didn't want to get yelled at by these two, so I played dumb. Wasn't hard for me.

Zion took a seat across from us.

Another car pulled up.

The three of us waited silently.

In strode Ashley Moore.

Upon seeing him, Deliah's face lit up. She beckoned him to sit beside her. They were whispering to each other, which irritated Zion no end. "What are you two going on about? You're making more noise than a couple of screeching mockingbirds."

"Mind your own business," Ashley warned.

"Or what?" Zion countered.

Realizing that Zion was unnerved by being in the room where Madison had died, I rose and sat beside him.

Zion barked, "Can you believe those two?"

"How have you been?"

Zion confessed, "Mostly drunk since Madison died."

"It will get better, I promise."

"I'll hold you to that."

Another car pulled up in front of Wickliffe Manor.

Deliah went to the window. "It's Robin and her husband."

Zion said, "I heard she was in the hospital."

"They must have released her," I said.

"She looks terrible," Deliah remarked before hurrying into the hallway.

With his arms around Robin, Peter helped her up the portico steps into the house. They paused momentarily in the hallway, getting their bearings as Zion had done.

Deliah rushed up to Robin and gave her a big hug. "Oh, Robin, I heard you were in the hospital."

Robin, still clinging to her husband and trying to push Deliah away, said, "I was released this morning."

"I'm so glad. You look great," Deliah gushed.

Zion and I exchanged glances, because Robin did look awful. There were dark circles under her eyes, her skin was the color of gray water, her unwashed hair hung in greasy strands, and she had lost a great deal of weight.

I leaned over and whispered, "See, things are looking up."

"Deliah was always good at comedy," Zion chimed in.

I repressed an urge to giggle. I guess it was the absurdity of Deliah's claim. What I did not find funny was that Ashley stayed in his seat when Robin came in.

Wasn't Robin his birth mother? Why did he not greet her—a woman so obviously ill?

I saw Robin notice that Ashley was in the parlor, and her face fell when he did not rise to greet her—the jerk.

Both Zion and I got up and went over to Robin.

Seeing us, Peter groused, "This is beyond belief." He handed us the note.

"We all got one," Zion confided.

"I need to take Robin home. She's not feeling well."

Robin shushed Peter. "No, honey. I wanted to come. This must be about Madison." She looked at me expectantly.

I nodded. "Sit over here, Robin. Might as well make yourself comfortable." I extended my hand toward a chair.

"This better be fast. Robin needs her rest," Peter growled.

John walked into the room. Upon seeing Zion, he paused, but then strode over to Robin. "Feeling better, Robin?"

"Yes, much. I know I don't look it, but I do feel much better. John, thank you for the beautiful flowers. They were lovely."

John bent over and kissed Robin's hand. "Beautiful flowers for a beautiful lady."

Robin blushed. It was the first hint of color since she had entered in the room.

"Hi, Peter," John greeted.

"Yes, thank you for the flowers. Robin enjoyed them very much," Peter replied.

John sat down after greeting Deliah and Ashley while ignoring Zion and me.

Deliah plopped down next to him, and pretended to be enthralled with whatever John uttered.

Zion paced the room while I fidgeted impatiently in my seat. I wanted to get this show on the road.

Hearing footfalls on the grand staircase, everyone grew quiet. Into the parlor walked Franklin with his hands in his pockets. Behind him strode Hunter.

John jumped up and pointed at Franklin. "What is this about? Why is he here?"

"Because I asked Franklin to be here, as I did all of you," Asa said, pushing past the brothers. "Please sit, gentlemen."

"I will not!" John complained. "This is unseemly. First, I am accosted by a goon who threatened and forced me to come back to this wretched house. Now I have to share the same room with my wife's murderer. This is too much. Too much."

Unperturbed by his outburst, Asa asked, "Mr. Smythe, don't you want to know who murdered your wife?"

"I know who killed my wife. That miserable little man," John Smythe said, pointing at Franklin.

Asa claimed, "Actually, Franklin didn't kill Miss

Madison, but the real perpetrator is sitting in this room."

"Ridiculous," scoffed John Smythe. "The police have him dead to rights."

"If you want to leave, you may, but I may end up accusing you for the murder of your wife."

John drew back, clearly astonished. "I wouldn't harm Madison. I loved her. Worshipped the ground she walked on."

"If you truly loved her, then stick round. That goes for all of you. I'm not going to hold anyone against their will, but the name of the murderer will be revealed in a few minutes," Asa said.

"What's she saying?" Robin asked her husband Peter.

"I'm not leaving," stated Zion, who plopped down on a chair with his arms folded. "We all know Franklin didn't kill Madison. Why would he? John had more motive than any of us."

I could tell by the way Zion and John looked at each other, we were going to have to separate those two before this was over.

John stomped his feet. "How dare you! How dare you!"

Asa shouted, "BE QUIET!"

Everyone stopped chattering and gave Asa their full attention.

"That's better. Franklin and Hunter, please be seated."

Shaking with excitement, Deliah pointed with a forefinger tipped by an extremely long fingernail with blue glitter fingernail polish. "You're the lady who bought the expensive cookware from me. I got a huge commission."

"It's gratifying that you remember me." Asa looked around the group. "Let me introduce myself. My name is Asa Reynolds, and I've been asked by Franklin's legal counsel to look into Madison Smythe's demise."

Ashley asked, "Your last name is Reynolds? Are you any relation to Josiah?"

"She's my daughter," I said.

Ashley guffawed, "Whatever we hear will be a biased rehearsal for the trial. We all know Josiah and Franklin are the best of friends. Of course Josiah's daughter is going to proclaim Franklin innocent."

"Perhaps," Asa said calmly. "It doesn't mean I'm wrong. I can prove that a person present in this room murdered Madison Smythe, and that it wasn't Franklin."

Deliah looked downcast. "Then you don't own a horse farm, do you? You don't want to act in our little theater group. You lied to me."

Bemused at Deliah's naivety, Asa said, "I'm a troubleshooter. Companies and people with lots of money hire me to take care of problems that are best kept quiet and out of the public eye. Mainly theft and fraud."

Ashley spoke up, "So you're not the police. I don't know why we're staying for this charade. This woman has no power over us." He rose.

Zion threatened, "Sit down, boy."

"This woman has no authority."

Zion glared at Ashley. "I'm gonna tell you one more time. Sit down, or I'll break your skull wide open." He looked hopefully at Asa, who was standing in the middle of the circle of chairs. "You know who killed Madison?"

"I do, sir."

"Can you prove it?"

"Yes, I can."

Zion threatened, "No one is leaving this room until the lady is finished."

"This is just like the play we were going to perform where all the suspects are gathered in Lady Elton's ballroom, and Detective Weatherby uncovers the real murderer," Deliah rhapsodized, her eyes bright.

Disgusted, Hunter spoke up. "This is no play, Miss Deliah. An innocent woman was killed in my house. I want to know who did it and bring him to justice."

"Your brother killed my wife. I don't care what trick this woman is trying to pull," John snarled.

"Let's start with you, Mr. Smythe," Asa ventured.

John drew back in his chair. "Me?"

"You keep insisting Franklin murdered your wife because of the bad blood between them. Let's start with the evidence, shall we? You filled the goblets that night. Did you fill them from the cranberry juice bottle or the decanter?"

"Let me think now."

"Don't be cagey, Mr. Smythe. Your police statement said, and I quote, 'I took the decanter from the refrigerator and filled the goblets already on the table. I placed the decanter on the table as well. I later saw Franklin dusting the table, having removed the decanter and goblets.'"

"That sounds right. Yes, that's what I said."

"Whose job was it to fill the decanter and goblets?"

"Franklin's, I guess."

"He was the props manager, wasn't he?"

"Yeessss."

"It was his job to fill the goblets?"

John took a handkerchief from his pocket and wiped his forehead.

Asa asked again, "Whose job was it to fill the decanter and goblets?"

"Franklin's."

"Had you ever filled the goblets before?"

"No."

"Then why, on the night of your wife's death, did you take it upon yourself to fill them?"

Zion suddenly leapt from his chair, wrapping his hands around John's neck. "You killed her! You killed her!"

Franklin and Hunter jumped up and pulled Zion away from John, who was gasping for air as he slid to the floor. Hunter shoved Zion into his chair, warning, "Do not move from that seat again."

Asa helped John back into his chair. "You're all right, Mr. Smythe."

"I think I need a doctor."

"No, you don't, Mr. Smythe. Let's continue. Why on this particular night did you fill the goblets?"

"I wanted to start rehearsal and saw they weren't filled, so I did it myself. That's all there was to it. I swear to God, there was no other reason." He began wheezing. "I do think I need a doctor."

"You're feeling adrenaline kicking in, Mr. Smythe. That's all. Let's move on to the script. Where did you get the manuscript for *The Murder Trap*?"

"I purchased it from an internet agency that handles copyrighted plays."

"Did you have to pay royalties to use the play?"

"Yes, but the fee was nominal."

"So you purchased the right to use *The Murder Trap* script from an agency?"

"Correct."

"Did you make any changes to the script?"

"No. I would never do that. The play is good. Doesn't need any fixing."

Asa picked up a copy of the script from a side table and handed it to John. "Is this one of the scripts distributed to the cast?"

John thumbed through it, coughing now and then. "It's Madison's copy. That's her handwriting in the margins."

"It is indeed your wife's copy. Now, will you turn to page seventeen, please?"

Deliah took the manuscript from John and opened to page seventeen before handing the manuscript back.

"Are you on page seventeen, Mr. Smythe?"

"Yes."

"Will you please read out loud the stage instructions for the protagonist, which was played by Miss Madison, as to which goblet she was to drink from."

John took out bifocals from a case in his pocket and put the glasses on. Using his finger, he found the passage Asa requested. "It reads that the leading lady is to pick up the goblet from the left."

"And you still maintain that nothing was changed from the original manuscript you received from the agency?"

"I already told you, nothing was changed."

Asa picked up two more scripts and handed one to Zion and the other to Ashley. "How do you explain that these scripts have no such instructions regarding which goblet the female protagonist is to drink from? One I purchased from the agency, and the other one downloaded off the internet."

Deliah snatched the script from Ashley and flipped

through until she came to page seventeen. "There are no such instructions in this rendition of the play. John, did you put those instructions into the script?"

"Mr. Foley, what about your copy of the script?" Asa asked, walking in a circle with her head bowed.

Zion threw the heavy, bound script on the floor. "No such instruction in this one either."

John remained silent, using the time to carefully consider his answer. Finally, he spoke, "It's true that I made a few little changes here and there, but Madison was having difficulty remembering stage directions and her lines. I was trying to help, that's all."

"I told you he did it," Zion accused.

"Mr. Foley, please restrain yourself," my daughter said.

"What motive did I have to kill Madison?" asked John, looking helplessly about the room.

Zion started to speak, but I pinched him to keep quiet.

Asa replied, "I can think of two motives: one is money and the other is jealousy. It has been reported to me that it was Miss Madison who held the purse strings, and you had signed a disadvantageous prenup that would leave you penniless if the two of you divorced."

"I loved her."

"Then there was the fact she was having an affair with someone in this group."

Robin sat straighter in her chair at that little bombshell.

"It was nothing," John replied.

Deliah blurted out, "I saw Madison kiss another man upstairs, and when you discovered them, there was a scuffle. I heard her say she wanted a divorce."

John sneered, "Aren't you the little snoop!"

I think he would have scratched Deliah's eyes out if we hadn't been around.

Frightened, Deliah scooted in her chair away from him.

Asa continued, "Miss Deliah, can you identify the man you saw kissing Miss Madison upstairs?"

"It was Zion."

"Mr. Foley, can you confirm?" asked Asa, standing in front of John and blocking his view of Zion.

"Madison and I were in love, and she wanted a divorce, but not because of us. She just wanted to get away from John."

"Oh, you poor sap," laughed John. "You were the last of a long list of suckers Madison played. She loved the drama of an affair. She loved the attention. Don't flatter yourself, pal. Madison never loved you. She was never going to leave me. It was the same routine over and over again. Madison would entice a man to fall for her, contrive for them to get caught, cause a scene, say she wanted a divorce, then when tired of the idiot, she'd dump him."

I felt Zion stiffen in his chair next to me. His brow broke out into a sweat while his eyelids fluttered.

"Hunter," I called out.

Hunter rushed over and felt Zion's pulse. "Franklin, get me some aspirin. Quick!"

Franklin hurried into the kitchen and returned with a bottle of aspirin and a glass of water.

Hunter gave Zion four aspirins and checked his pulse again. "I think we need to get you to the hospital, old man."

Zion pushed Hunter's hand away. "Thank you, but no. I'm going to see this through. It's a panic attack. I have them all the time. They look like heart attacks, but I've been checked out. My heart is strong and sound."

Hunter addressed Asa. "Well?"

"Mr. Foley's a big boy. He knows the risks. If he wants to stay, let him."

Reluctantly, Hunter went back to his seat, as did Franklin.

I leaned over to Zion. "You let me know the moment you feel any worse. Promise."

Zion nodded as Asa continued.

"Mr. Smythe, so far we have established that you had both motive and opportunity."

"So did everyone else. What about Zion? Madison probably told him they were through, and he killed her in a rage," John accused.

"That is a possibility." Asa turned her attention to

Zion. "Did Miss Madison call it off with you?"

"Never. And even if Madison had, I never would have hurt her. To destroy all that loveliness would have been a sin."

Asa harrumphed as she took a small scrap of paper off a table, handing it to Zion. "Do you recognize this note? And please read out loud."

Zion took the note and read, "Darling, we'll be together soon."

"Do you know who wrote this note?"

"I did."

"Did you try to disguise your cursive handwriting on this note?"

"No."

Asa turned and winked at Hunter. "Whom was this note intended for?"

"Madison."

"How did you give it to her?"

"I left love notes in her coat pockets."

"Did you do this often?"

"Yes."

"When did you leave this particular note?"

"On the night of her death."

"When you stuffed these notes in her pockets, did you ever discover any other items?"

Zion looked away.

"Mr. Foley? Did you find other items in her coat pockets?"

"I would find small items."

"Such as?" Asa inquired.

"Just bits and pieces."

Asa walked around the room. "Perhaps a pair of sterling silver salt and pepper shakers? Or a valuable first edition of *Leaves of Grass*? Things like that—small, but valuable to a collector?"

Zion nodded, wiping away a tear.

I handed him one of my good linen handkerchiefs—again.

"What did you do with the things you discovered in Miss Madison's pockets?"

"I realized they were from Wickliffe Manor, so I would put them back if I could. Franklin noticed items were missing, so he started surreptitiously checking people's tote bags and coats. He discovered something in Madison's coat, and after that, I had a hard time retrieving items from her pockets before Franklin got to them."

"Did you ask Miss Madison about the items?"

"She said she didn't take them, and that's all she would say about it."

Asa swiveled on her high heels. "Is that because Miss Madison was covering up for you, Mr. Smythe?"

Before John could reply, Robin chimed in, "I saw him take a jade statuette off a side table at Wickliffe Manor and stuff it in Madison's coat pocket." She looked around at everyone. "I did. I saw him take it."

Asa asked, "Mr. Smythe, do you have a problem with sticky fingers?"

She held up a wagging finger. "Before you answer, I have several reports from high-end stores in Cincinnati, Louisville, and Nashville from which you have been banned."

John's shoulders slumped. "When I'm anxious, I take little things. It helps with my anxiety. I don't know why I do it. It calms me. Madison would always cover for me. 'Don't worry, John,' she'd say. 'I'll smooth everything over,' and she did. Madison was kind like that."

John regarded Franklin. "Madison tried to put your things back, but I kept stealing faster than she could keep up with. When you confronted her, Franklin, she was mortified. Madison cried, saying I had shamed her, and she didn't know how was she going to face people."

"She never explained your situation to me, John," Franklin said.

"Madison would never have exposed me. That's the kind of person she was. She went to her grave keeping my secret."

"The noose seems to be tightening around your neck, Mr. Smythe," Asa said. "You filled the goblets that contained ethylene glycol. You knew your wife was having an affair. You were stealing from Wickliffe Manor and having your wife cover for you."

John slid off his chair to the floor onto his knees imploring, "I didn't do it. I didn't do it. I swear to God I didn't do it."

Asa smiled. "No, Mr. Smythe, you didn't."

"What?" John squeaked, gaping up at Asa.

"I know you didn't kill your wife."

"You believe me?"

"Please get back into your seat."

Asa handed out nine identical photographs. "These are copies of a police photograph taken of the decanter and the goblets. Do you concur?"

Everyone nodded, including me.

"Was it possible that someone tampered with either the decanter or the goblets after Miss Madison fell ill?"

Franklin spoke up. "No. Seven of us in this room were always present after Madison became ill. If someone tampered with the decanter and goblets, one of us would have seen it, and I always marked the juice bottle when I poured the juice into the decanter. It was at the level I had marked, and both the decanter and goblets had not been disturbed. After she died, Hunter closed off the room. No one went back in there until the paramedics arrived."

"Why did you close off the room, Mr. Wickliffe?"

"Mrs. Smythe has passed. There was nothing more to be done. I did it out of respect."

"Does everyone agree with Franklin and Hunter's assessment?"

We all nodded or murmured yes.

"Then look at the photograph and tell me if you notice something odd about the decanter and the goblets."

Everyone carefully examined their copy of the photograph and remained puzzled. Deliah turned hers upside down while studying it. Ashley put his aside. John and Zion regarded the photograph intently. Robin looked at hers and then handed it to her husband Peter.

"How did Madison ingest the antifreeze?" asked Asa, disappointed that no one had made the connection.

Zion spoke up. "From drinking the cranberry juice."

"You assumed she ingested the antifreeze from the cranberry juice. Franklin has already stated that he marked the juice bottle after he poured the juice into the decanter."

"But antifreeze was found in the cranberry juice," John insisted.

"That is correct, Mr. Smythe," Asa replied. "Yet, how do we know Miss Madison ingested it from the cranberry juice?"

Deliah turned her picture right side up and studied it. "I've got it! I know!" she shouted.

"Miss Deliah, you have the floor," Asa said, grinning.

"Look at the goblets. See? They're full to the brim.

No one drank out of the goblets," Deliah pointed out.

"Let's take it step by step. Franklin always marked the level of juice in the bottle. He poured the juice into the decanter, marked the level of juice on the bottle, and put both the bottle and decanter into the fridge. Are you with me?"

I nodded along with everyone else.

"Mr. Smythe came along and took the decanter into the parlor. We know he didn't tamper with the level of liquid in the juice bottle because Franklin witnessed him taking the decanter out of the fridge and carrying it into the parlor, where Franklin witnessed Mr. Smythe pouring the juice from the decanter into the goblets. Mr. Smythe went to another part of the house, and Franklin decided to take the decanter and goblets off the table and dust. He then put the decanter and goblets back.

"Now watch this." Asa pointed to an end table, which held a decanter and two goblets similar to the ones used in the play. "As you can see, the goblets are full and the decanter is filled three-fourths of the way to the top. Now if I pour the contents of the goblets back into the decanter, what do I have?" Asa poured the juice from the goblets into the decanter.

Deliah bounced up and down on her chair. "You have the decanter filled to the level Franklin had marked!"

"Correct." Asa turned toward Franklin. "How much

juice did you pour into the decanter?"

"I filled it all the way to the top."

"When Mr. Smythe took the decanter into the parlor, what was the level of liquid in the decanter?"

"The decanter was filled to the top."

"And after he poured into the goblets?"

"John poured out enough juice for two goblets."

The room went quiet, with each person silent in their thoughts.

"I think we have proven that Madison Smythe was not poisoned by the cranberry juice, since we can account for every drop of juice that fateful night."

Ashley snarled, "Then who put poison in the cranberry juice and when?"

"Good question. I would suggest that it was done to throw us off the actual way Miss Madison ingested the ethylene glycol."

"We're right back where we started," Robin complained.

"Be patient, Miss Robin. We're almost there," advised Asa. "All of you were asked by the police to have your doctor check for calcium oxalate crystals, which are deposited in the kidneys after exposure to ethylene glycol. Mother, do you have calcium oxalate crystals in your kidneys?"

"No, I don't."

"Franklin?"

"No."

"Hunter."

Hunter shook his head.

"Miss Deliah?"

"My doctor said I was in perfect health," Deliah replied, smiling and throwing out her chest.

"Mr. Moore?"

"Nope."

"Mr. Smythe?"

"No sign of those crystals."

"Mr. Foley?"

Zion looked nervously at Asa. "Yes."

"Say that again."

"Yes, my doctor found crystals, and I have been treated for the condition."

"I see. That leaves Miss Robin." Asa walked over and stood in front of Robin Russell. "Do you have calcium oxalate crystals concentrated in your kidneys?"

"I did. Massive amounts, the doctor said. That's what was causing my confusion, and then my body threatened to shut down completely. My doctor said I would have been dead in another forty-eight hours. I was lucky. Very lucky." Smiling, Robin turned to Peter and held his hand.

Asa walked around the circle, making contact with all nine sets of eyes. "So, out of the entire theater group, three people display signs of having ingested antifreeze—Madison Smythe, Zion Foley, and Robin Russell. How did they ingest it? What did these three people have in common? The answer is the theater group, where all three were poisoned when the group met to rehearse."

The grandfather clock sounded in the hallway. Ashley took a quick look at his watch. "It's on the hour," he announced.

Robin seemed aghast. "But who and why?"

"Before we get to that, some dirty laundry needs to be tidied up." Asa picked up a report from a side table.

"Mr. Moore, why did you come to Lexington?"

"For school."

"You are from northern Kentucky, are you not?"

"Yes."

"There are good colleges there and across the river in Cincinnati."

"I felt I needed to be here."

"Why was that?"

"None of your business. Look, I'm getting sick of this."

"You *are* going the long way around the barn, Miss Reynolds," Zion commented.

"I'll get to the point, then," Asa replied. "You came to Lexington to search for your birth mother. Correct?"

Ashley glanced at Robin. "How is that relevant to this murder case?"

Undeterred, Asa asked, "You are adopted, are you not?"

"Maybe I am. What's that got to do with this?"

"In fact, you joined this theater group to be close to your birth mother."

Robin shot me a look of utter despair, but I was not going to interfere. The umbilical cord had to be severed.

Ashley was silent.

"You won't expound on this?"

Robin jumped to Ashley's defense. "I'm his mother." She turned to Peter. "I wanted to tell you, but my mind got so muddled."

Shocked, Peter pulled away from Robin's embrace.

"Please understand," she begged. "I was so very young at the time."

Asa picked up another report and turned to Ashley. "Is Miss Robin your mother?"

"Yes."

"How do you know?"

"I saw my birth certificate after my adoptive father passed away."

"I have a copy of Ashley Moore's birth certificate. Can you verify that this is your birth certificate?"

Ashley took the certificate, perused it, and handed it back. "It is my birth certificate."

"Are you positive?"

"Of course I'm sure," Ashley snapped.

Asa picked up another report on the table and handed it to Robin. "Miss Robin, while you were in the hospital, my mother paid you a visit."

"Josiah was nice enough to visit and bring a bouquet."

"I'm glad you acknowledge that my mother Josiah was there. Besides wanting to see how you were doing, I wanted her to pick up something for me."

"I'm sorry, Robin, but I took hair from your hairbrush and replaced your used toothbrush with a new one," I confessed.

"Whatever for, Josiah?"

"So we could obtain a DNA sample," Asa answered.

Outraged, Peter barked, "That's an invasion of my wife's privacy. It is certainly illegal as well."

Asa turned to Ashley. "We also got a sample of your DNA, Ashley."

"What?" Ashley froze in his seat.

"You tossed a styrofoam coffee cup out on the street. One of my men, who was following you, picked it up."

"What are you trying to do here? Hurt my wife?" Peter fired at Asa.

She handed the DNA report to Robin. "Would you like to read the results, Miss Robin?"

Ashley jumped up and ran, but was blocked by Detective Kelly, who stepped in from the hallway.

We all stood except for Robin, who was reading the report. Silently, it drifted from her hands onto the floor.

Kelly entered the room and backed Ashley into his chair.

"Thank you, Detective," Asa said. "You all recognize Detective Kelly. He and several of his colleagues have been listening in the hall. We suspected someone might make a run for it."

Hunter acquired another chair and beckoned Kelly to sit.

Kelly nodded and took his place in the circle.

Asa smiled. "Detective Kelly will be joining us for the duration of our get-together. Everyone, please take your seats again."

"I don't understand. Why would you do such a thing?" Robin implored Ashley.

He refused to look at her.

"What did the report say?" Deliah asked as she picked it up from the floor. She scanned it, her face growing pale.

"Please read the results from the DNA test," Asa instructed.

Deliah looked with great tenderness at Robin, who was quietly weeping. "It says that Ashley and Robin are no match. Ashley is not Robin's son."

All eyes turned upon Ashley.

"Ashley, would you care to explain why you contacted Robin Russell and claimed to be her son?"

"I was mistaken about the identity of my birth mother. Sorry, Robin."

"Tsk, tsk, Ashley. Is that your real name?"

"Of course it is."

"Remember the cup you threw on the ground? You threw other items on the ground as well, and they were all picked up by my people. You're quite the litterbug, Ashley. Odd behavior for a person whose room is so clean. Almost OCD clean . . . and what's up with the lock? Was it because you felt your roommates might sneak into your bedroom and stumble across the fact that you weren't Ashley Moore?"

Ashley's eyes widened. "You're the woman who I caught in my room. You bitch!"

"Sticks and stones," Asa said, grinning. "Where was I?"

Detective Kelly offered, "You were telling Ashley that his bad habit of littering our fair city proved to be a boon for the police."

"Thank you, Detective Kelly." Asa picked up another report from the sideboard. "Ashley, I took your trash to the good detective here, and he arranged for a fingerprint analysis after I showed him the DNA report. He ran your prints through the FBI's AFIS system."

Ashley groaned.

"Your real name is Robert Warren Biddle," Asa confirmed.

"You're the cause of this. I'm not going to take the rap for you!" Ashley yelled.

"Who's he shouting at?" Franklin asked, looking around the room.

Asa stood before Peter Russell. "Ashley is talking to you, isn't he, Peter?"

"Asa, stop. You're going too far with this," Robin said. "Peter, tell her she's got the wrong man."

Asa gently took Robin's arm and tried to pull her away from her husband.

Several uniformed policemen entered the room and stood behind Peter.

"Peter!" Robin cried, clinging to him.

"Mother," Asa beckoned.

Both Franklin and I went over to Robin and led her to a couch in the corner of the room.

"I'm so sorry, Robin," I said, trying to comfort her.

"Get away from me," Robin hissed. "You're trying to pin Madison's death on Peter."

I felt awful. How do you tell a woman that her life has just shifted into the crap zone? I've been there. I know how it feels.

"Madison wasn't the target for murder, Robin. It was you," I said.

"You're crazy," Robin insisted.

"This can't be happening!" Ashley whined.

Asa said to Ashley, "You want to give it up?"

"Don't," warned Peter. "As long as you keep quiet, the police have nothing."

Ashley spoke. "I was his student. I was broke, and

he knew it."

"To whom are you referring?" Detective Kelly asked.

"Peter Russell."

"Shut up," Peter growled. "Shut up."

Ashley sang like a bird. "He told me he wanted to play a joke on his wife. Some joke."

"What were your instructions?" Detective Kelly asked.

"I was to play up to Robin. You know, be nice and get her attention."

"Get Robin to like you?" Asa asked.

"Exactly. That was part of it. Then he told me about the kid she had at fifteen, and I was to convince her that I was her long-lost son."

Robin asked, "Peter, how did you even know I had a son as a teenager?"

"I'm saying nothing."

"Go on," Asa urged Ashley.

"On the night Madison died, Peter met me in a parking lot before rehearsal and gave me a vial of liquid. He said it was vodka mixed with sugar. He wanted me to pour it into the juice bottle. It was to get everyone tipsy and then I was to take pictures. It was to be a practical joke."

The room was silent, probably because no one believed Ashley's explanation. No one could be that dumb.

Asa broke the silence with her question, "Did you mix the liquid with the cranberry juice?"

"I was late, so I put some in the goblets, the decanter, and finally the juice bottle when no one was looking."

"How do you explain that your fingerprints weren't on these items?"

"I used the bottom of my t-shirt to lift the decanter top and unscrew the juice bottle. The goblets didn't have a top, so I just put a few drops in each glass. Listen, if Madison didn't drink from the goblets, I'm in the clear. I didn't have anything to do with her murder."

Asa declared, "Mr. Russell's right about one thing. Do shut up."

"This kid's crazy. Look, he came to me and threatened to blackmail my wife, so I went along with him to keep him quiet. All this stuff about me hiring him is bunk."

"I believe it's referred to as a long con." I proposed.

Detective Kelly chortled, but restored his cop face before asking, "Would you like to add anything else, Mr. Russell?"

"I want a lawyer."

Deliah asked, "If Madison didn't drink any cranberry juice that night, where did she get the poison?"

"From Robin," I answered.

"That can't be, Josiah," Robin objected.

"I'm sorry, dear, it is, but you were being poisoned too. The poison in the cranberry juice was a red herring. Peter hoped Ashley would leave his fingerprints on the juice bottle to create a distraction for the police, while the massive dose of ethylene glycol was hidden in your thermos."

"You bastard!" yelled Ashley. "You were trying to frame me for murder!"

Ignoring Ashley's outburst, I continued. "Ethylene glycol metabolizes into oxalic acid and combines with calcium in the body to form calcium oxalate crystals which are deposited in the kidneys. We know only Madison, Zion, and Robin had these crystals in their systems. Why? Because Robin, in a gesture of goodwill, shared her sangria with them during rehearsals. It was their little secret."

Zion agreed. "That's right. Robin always brought enough alcohol for us to share throughout rehearsal."

John added, "I would surmise Madison's behavior was difficult because the poison made her sick."

Deliah leaned forward in her seat. "But why is Madison dead and not Robin?"

Asa took the lead on this question. "I guess Robin had built up some immunity to it over time, and Peter didn't realize that ethanol in wine and hard liquor neutralizes ethylene glycol. I suspect Peter realized his mistake and put a massive dose of it in the thermos that night, and Madison drank more of it than Robin."

"I'm going to sue each and every one of you for defiling my good name," Peter threatened. "You can't prove a thing."

"But we can, Peter. I got suspicious when you kept trying to get Robin to drink a milkshake you brought to the hospital. When she wouldn't drink it, you poured it out into the toilet and then rinsed out the container."

"I wanted Robin's room to be neat," Peter spluttered.

"Yeah. What you don't know, Peter, is that I waited until you left and snuck back into Robin's room, retrieving the milkshake container along with Robin's hair from her comb and her toothbrush. She was asleep, remember, so Robin didn't see me."

Peter gave a chilling smile and said, "Any such evidence would be inadmissible in court."

"It's funny that you haven't asked what was found in the milkshake container, but then again, you already know. Antifreeze," I said.

"But antifreeze is green. The liquid he gave me was clear," Ashley asserted.

"Antifreeze is dyed green, but its main component, ethylene glycol, is colorless," Detective Kelly said. "One of its many uses is to replace formaldehyde as a preservative for biological specimens. Don't you teach biology, Mr. Russell?"

Peter snarled, "Screw you!"

"We took the liberty of searching your office and

lab at the university while your wife was being discharged from the hospital this morning. We found invoices for ethylene glycol and several partially empty bottles of it. What we found to be most interesting was a life insurance policy on your wife for five hundred thousand dollars taped under your desk drawer." Kelly pulled out his handcuffs. "Stand up, please. You are under arrest for the murder of Madison Smythe and the attempted murder of Robin Russell and Zion Foley."

Kelly cuffed Peter and spun him around to face him. "This is a real pleasure to book you. Boys, take him out and make sure you 'Mirandize' Mr. Russell. We don't want this guy to get off because of any legal technicalities."

Hunter rushed over and clapped Franklin on the back. "It's over, brother."

"Thank goodness."

Asa went over to Deliah and handed her a business card. "Call me if you get tired of selling cookware. I have a place for a gal with such obvious assets," she said, referring to Deliah's ample breasts. "But if you do want to work for me, cut out the dumbbell act. Smart women should never play stupid."

Deliah grinned and, grabbing the card, shoved it into her cleavage. "I'll think about it."

I searched for Zion and Robin.

Both were sitting, stunned.

John was bending over Robin and speaking to her

in low tones. He helped her to her feet while grabbing her purse.

"Where're you going, John?" I asked.

"I'm driving Robin home and calling her doctor. I think she's in shock."

"Then what?"

"I'm going to stay with Robin until someone in her family arrives. We both have suffered the loss of our spouses. I think it's time for healing. Perhaps we can help each other."

Robin reached out to me. "Why? Why did he do it?"

"You said you were having financial problems, Robin. This was Peter's way of solving them."

John said, "Come on, Robin. I'm taking you home. We can talk all night long if you wish." They passed by me—two broken people hanging on to each other to keep from drowning.

I went to the window, watching John put Robin in his car and drive off.

Zion followed as well, sneaking out without speaking to anyone.

Asa came up behind me and put her arm around my shoulder.

We sadly watched the police put Ashley in one police car and Peter in another.

"What do you always say about justice, Mom?"

"There's justice, and then there's Kentucky justice."

"I've always wondered what you meant by it."

"Justice is not always found in a courtroom."

"It will be this time."

"I hope so. If not, Zion will be waiting."

"What do you mean?"

"One of the items I found in Zion's briefcase was a revolver. I think Zion was planning to kill John with it, but now that he knows Peter is the real culprit, he'll be waiting for him."

"Let's hope the jury convicts Peter."

"Yes, let's," I agreed.

Kentucky is a dark and bloody ground, thick with the blood of both heroes and villains.

Don't . . . ever . . . let . . . your . . . guard . . . down!